THE BOY WHO W

Book One

The Sword in the Stone

A Novel by Jeffery L. VanMeter

2015 Tastefully Twisted Publications

The Sword in the Stone

Long ago in a time few remember, the land was divided and had no King.

The trouble began when the Lady of the Lake decided to build a closer connection between the people of the Earthly Realm with the world of Magic and the Spirits of the Woods and Water. She believed that bringing the two closer together would bring stability and peace.

And so she sent the Igrain, a Lady of the Island of Avalon where no man had before had ever stepped foot upon to the Land of Men to marry one of the powerful Lords.

Contests were held so that Igrain could choose one from among the many Knights and Lords who would prove himself the strongest, the bravest and the wisest of all Men.

Most represented themselves with honor and fidelity in these contests. But she underestimated the greed and lust for power of the Lords and Knights of the Land.

Most of the men who owned land and controlled large territories thought only of themselves and thought little of the people who it was their responsibility to lead with strength and wisdom.

Through bribery and deceit, the powerful Duke of Cornwall won the hand of Igrain. And before either the Lady of the Lake or the Wizard Merlin; who had long been the bridge between the Magical Realm and the World of Men discovered the false nature of the Duke, he had already spread his corruption across the Land and Igrain had born a daughter, Morgana.

The balance between the strength of the people and the wisdom of the Old Way of Spirits and Magic was offset by greed and the desire for wealth and power.

And so, the Lady of the Lake and Merlin decided that to restore the balance, a man whose strength and courage had to win out over all the rest. To him would be given the Sword of Power: Excalibur. He would become King and all the other Knights and Lords of the Land would swear their loyalty and fealty.

A way was discovered to rid the land of the curse of the Duke of Cornwall; unite the strength and courage of the King with the ancient wisdom brought to the Land with Igrain and secure a lasting peace.

For the right to wield the might sword Excalibur, the Lords and Knights gathered and for an entire year, they fought one another for the right to claim the prize. At sundown on the night of the winter solstice, Uther Pendragon proved to be the strongest; and at dawn the next morning, Merlin stood beside the Lake of Crystal Water and received Excalibur from the Lady of the Lake. The sword was given to Uther and all the Lords and Knights bowed to him as King.

But the something happened that the Lady and Merlin did not expect. They knew that Uther would fall in love with Igrain; but he was impatient.

He would not wait for Merlin and the Lady's plan to take shape. Breaking the alliance made with all the Lords and Knights, he laid siege to Seacrest, Cornwall's castle by the sea. For another year, he fought and failed against the walls of Seacrest. And so his desire for Igrain was so great, he begged Merlin to give him just one night with Igrain and swore on Excalibur to give Merlin whatever he asked in return.

That night, Uther withdrew his troops from Cornwall's castle and as the night settled into darkness, Cornwall took his troops to crush Uther's army as they slept.

But little did the Duke know that the clever Uther had set a trap for him and he would lead his troops into a slaughter. It was then that Merlin worked his magic, transforming Uther into the image of the Duke so that Uther could have his one night. As Uther spent the night with Igrain, Cornwall's army with the Duke at the head ran headlong into Uther's trap. The King's army was waiting for Cornwall and all but a few of Cornwall's army were slain, including the Duke himself.

Nine months later, Igrain gave birth to a son whom she named Arthur. Uther, knowing the child to be his own, married Igrain and vowed to raise him as his son. But on the day he first held his son, Merlin came to collect his due. Nothing is more sacred to a Knight than his word and so, honor-bound to keep his promise he took the child from Igrain and gave him to the Wizard.

As Igrain wept for the loss of her son, Uther went to pursue Merlin to bring back his child. He was nearly upon the Wizard, when enemies fell upon him. Uther fought bravely and with the power of Excalibur slew nearly all who attacked him.

In the battle, however he had suffered a mortal wound. At the top of a hill overlooking the field where Uther had won the right to be King, he knew he would soon die.

With his enemies still pursuing him, he vowed that no one but his own blood would have Excalibur. It was then that with his last breath leaving him he thrust the sword deep into a stone. His pursuers tried to pull the sword from its resting place, but all their attempts were futile.

The word then went across the land that he who could draw the sword from the stone would be King. For sixteen years, the strongest Lords and Knights of the land competed in a tournament for the right to attempt to draw the sword. Many Knights tried and all failed.

Until one day...

The Squire

Bors the Elder pulled himself out of the tent and stretched his aching body. As he did, he thought to himself that he didn't seem to remember traveling and camping on the side of the road taking so much of a toll.

"I guess I'm not nineteen anymore," he said to himself.

His son, Bors the Younger was curled up into a ball next to the still smoldering fire from the night before. He stepped over to the sleeping young man and rudely kicked him in the head.

"Get up, son. The road won't wait for us."

The young Knight groaned and rubbed his sleepy eyes as he sat up.

"It's barely even daylight," he complained.

"And if we're to make the tournament sight before sundown, we need to get moving."

Bors the Younger looked around and saw that most of the campsite was already packed and loaded onto the wagon. The horses were already saddled and everything needing to be done before moving on already finished. However, there was no fire going and no breakfast being cooked.

"Where's Arthur?" He whined. "I'm hungry."

Bors the Elder was curious about that as well. As he wondered about where his younger son could be, he heard the sound of someone coming out of the forest. He smiled and nodded as he recognized the sixteen year old Arthur entering the campsite with a fresh stag draped over his shoulders.

"Apparently he's been fetching our breakfast."

At seventeen, Arthur was already taller than his older brother. His long, blonde hair fell down in curls to his shoulders and he had a body molded by hard work in Bors the Elders' fields and stables. He brought the kill to where his brother was still seated on his blankets and dropped it in front of him.

"The next part's up to you," he told his brother with a wink.

The younger Bors looked at his father as if to complain, but found no sympathy there.

"Better get started," the older man told him. "I'm hungry."

"But why do I get to do the bloody work?" Bors the Younger whined.

Bors the Elder simply gave his son the familiar look of not being patient to hear any more dissent.

Before noon they were on their way to the fields of Surranam. While Arthur napped in the wagon, Bors the Elder and his first son rode proudly in front on two stallions. Bors the Elder had challenged many times for the right to try and draw the Sword from the stone. He'd even won three times, but was not strong enough for the Sword to even budge. But this was not his tournament at this time. His days of fighting for the right to be called King were behind him. This was to be his oldest son's first tournament. Although he doubted his son was ready to win, he knew that the boy needed the experience, even if it meant being taught a harsh lesson by a more seasoned warrior.

"Why does Arthur get to sleep while we ride?" Bors the Younger whined again.

"I'm not sure if you noticed," Arthur responded, "But I was up rather early this morning."

"So? That doesn't grant you any special privileges."

"Tell me," Arthur asked. "How hard was it for you getting the horses ready and packing the cart this morning?"

"You know right well I didn't do any of that."

"Precisely."

Bors the Elder scoffed and reminded his oldest son," Your brother's right. The ability to rest during a day when there's work to be done is a privilege that is earned and I'd definitely say that Arthur has well earned his rest."

"Well I skinned and butchered the stag. I don't get to take a nap for that."

"You're also not hungry are you?" Arthur added.

"You stay out of this. I'm talking to Father, not you."

"And apparently not getting the point," the Elder responded.

The sun was still hours from setting when Bors and his sons arrived at the tournament site. Looking at the field opened before them, Bors the Elder couldn't help a smile as he saw the banners of the Lords and Knights who had already arrived. The scarlet red banner with the white stallion of Uriants, the Duke of Westphalia was higher than the rest, but the Green Lion on the black field of Leon de Gras could still easily be seen as could the bees of Sunderland. To his surprise, he also recognized the Red Dragon of Cornwall.

"I thought the last Duke of Cornwall died years ago," Arthur commented.

"He did," Bors the Elder answered.

"Maybe the Duchess will be competing," the Younger said.

The Elder closed his eyes almost in an expression of pain as the sound of the comment felt like a slap across the face.

"I want you to think about that statement very carefully," he told his son.

"Do you think it might be her nephew Gawain?" Arthur asked.

"Quite possibly. He's just about old enough."

Bors the Elder felt like thumping his oldest son on the head when he asked, "If I help set up the campsite, do I get to take a nap?"

The younger Bors wasn't an idiot and knowing this made questions like those painful to hear. But he knew the lad had potential and would make a fine King were he to have the opportunity.

What would make him an even better King would be to have Arthur as his adviser. Arthur had a sharp mind and a quick wit. He'd also demonstrated an impressive ability to see things from other people's perspective; almost as if he could see the world through other's eyes. Any King having Arthur in his ear would be that much wiser.

Watching his sons practicing their sword technique also reminded Bors the Elder that Arthur would also make a fine Knight.

Bors the Younger was well-trained and more than capable; but Arthur was faster, stronger and much more clever. His particular style was to use his opponent's aggression against him. As the two boys sparred, he noticed Arthur blocking and parrying his brother's strikes patiently until his foe would overcommit. After the older son would invariably strike too eagerly and lose his balance, Arthur would simply let his brother miss and slap him on the rear.

"You lost your balance again," Arthur teased his brother.

"Father…" The Younger complained.

"Your brother's right," The Elder answered. "You have to learn to be more patient."

As the two boys readied themselves for another round, the Elder Bors reminded his eldest, "And don't try to overpower your enemy. You'll only tire yourself sooner."

As their wooden swords once again danced with each other, Bors the Elder felt saddened that he couldn't make Arthur a Knight. The tradition that all noblemen adhered to was that if a Count, like himself were to have two sons, the first son would be the one Knighted and the second son his squire. But even in the event of a third son being born, only one of the sons could be Knighted.

Higher ranking Lords such as a Duke or an Earl could have as many Knights as they could afford to pay. The Barons could have as many as four Knights; but no more.

He felt guilty for thinking that Arthur may have been the better warrior and more intelligent; especially considering the origins he'd kept secret for sixteen years. In a better world, he thought Arthur should have the right to claim his true father's title and privileges. But that was not to be. He swore to the Wizard that Arthur would never know.

Arthur

Arthur himself could care less who would become King. That wasn't his concern. However this was still his favorite time of year as it was another chance to see the two friends he'd known since being small, Gawain and Betivere.

It didn't take him long to find Betivere. He was walking about the campsite with his staff among the continually growing throngs. A makeshift town square had sprouted up with merchants selling their wares to the people who would make up a small city for the next three days.

Arthur crept along as quietly as he could behind his friend, making sure to stay in the "sound shadow" (as his father called it) of others. He could barely resist a laugh as he crept closer and closer; until suddenly, just as he reached out his hand to touch the young man, he felt Betivere's staff on his inner thigh.

"When was the last time you had a bath?" Betivere teased.

"So it was my delicious aroma that gave me away this time, was it?" Arthur asked.

Betivere turned around showing a wry smile under the swollen mass around his eyes.

"If you look as bad as you smell right now, thank God I'm mostly blind."

Betivere was the son of the Earl of Sunderland. His favorite hobby was beekeeping and the skin around his eyes had been stung so often, his face was swollen to the point where he was practically blind.

It was said of him though that he had a kind of "Inner sight" that allowed him to look into people's hearts and no matter how limited his sight was, he had learned to use his other senses to compensate.

"So how's the year been to you?" Arthur asked him.

"It's been fair," Betivere answered. "I would have some complaints, but I doubt anyone would want to hear them."

The two walked around the campsite laughing and remembering old times when they eventually came upon Gawain, the nephew of the Duchess of Cornwall. Arthur nearly gasped at the site of him as unlike the previous years, this time Gawain was wearing ring mail, leather and the tunic of a Knight.

"Well, it's about time!" Arthur said happily. "It is official? Has she named you as her heir?"

"Did the sun rise in the north this morning?" Gawain answered in his husky voice. "Uriants of Westphalia Knighted me after I chased down two men who had raped a young woman."

"When did this happen?" Arthur asked, impressed.

"Two...three months ago. I'm still not sure. I was escorting my cousin Morgana to Westphalia and word came from one of the villages that a woman had been raped and to be on the watch for two men in armor. When I arrived at Barrimore, I found two men who fit the description of the rapists training alongside the rest of Uriants's troops."

"Let me guess," Betivere interrupted. "You accused them and they fell to their knees in repentance."

"Nothing in my life is ever that easy," Gawain continued. "I brought it up to Lord Uriants and he summoned the two men so he could question them. Obviously, they knew they couldn't get away with trying to lie to Lord Uriants..."

"Yes," Arthur added. "It's that whole being able to smell a lie thing he has."

"So they ran. For some reason..."

Arthur saw her out of the corner of his eye at first. The sight was so stunning, he simply could not resist his full attention falling upon her. Gawain continued with his heroic story, but Arthur was no longer able to pay any attention to anything other than the most beautiful girl he'd ever seen (or at least that day).

Her hair was a soft brown and braided into a long tail extending halfway down her back. She was slender, but not malnourished Arthur thought; she had subtle curves but was far from buxom. Everything about her seemed perfectly proportionate.

But it was the smile that seized Arthur's attention the most. With her round, brown eyes sparkling in the sunlight, her smile told of both a sweetness and a little of the spice of wit. Not only could Arthur say of her that she was lovely, he guessed that she was likely at least as clever as himself.

"Did you hear that?" Betivere asked.

"Hear what?" Gawain answered.

"I'm not entirely sure, but I think I heard a lightning bolt strike poor Arthur right in the middle of the chest."

"What? How can you tell? You're supposed to be blind."

"There's only one thing that could cause Arthur's heart to start pounding so fast or his breath to so quicken."

"And if he doesn't close his mouth soon it will be full of flies in a minute," Gawain added.

Suddenly the girl glanced over at the three of them and rewarded them with a sweet, but also playfully clever expression.

"Perhaps you should paint a portrait," she said to Arthur, "It may last longer."

"No painting could ever capture the true beauty of a rose in bloom," Arthur responded.

The young lady look impressed and continued with the famous poem.

"No paint on canvass could have her fragrance of spring..."

"Or the song of her voice," Arthur continued.

"Her delicate petals will never touch a lover's hand."

"Nor feel her breath upon him in a kiss."

"The painted rose has only the image of beauty."

"Her true beauty can never be merely seen."

"Well, well..." she said in a gently teasing voice, "It seems you've read a book or two."

As she turned to walk away, she added "Good for you."

Arthur was only barely aware that he'd started following her.

"I've read all the books in my father's library," he told her. "And some of the works in the monastery not far from Pembrook Castle."

"Oh don't tell me you stole from men of God."

"I prefer to think that I liberated them."

"From the house of God?"

"The Kingdom of God is within you and all around you," Arthur quoted. "Lift a stone and you will find me..."

The Lady stopped in her tracks and looked at Arthur in shock.

"Split a piece of wood and I am there," She said finishing the quote. "How can you know that? That's supposed to be..."

She then hurriedly covered her mouth as if to physically stop the words from escaping.

"I'm well aware that it's supposed to be forbidden knowledge," Arthur told her. "Which, of course leads to the question of how you came to knowledge of it?"

Her shocked expression faded and her warm, but teasing smile returned.

"You are the clever one aren't you?"

He followed her for about half an hour after that. She would challenge him with one question or another and he would answer with quotations from works and authors both popular and obscure.

She had to admit to herself that he was good looking. He was tall and strong and his face seemed to have a good balance of both sweetness and manly roughness.

His respectful manners and the fact that he had access to books seemed to indicate noble lineage. However, he clearly wasn't a Knight and as such she knew her father would never approve of her even talking to this young man.

But still, she thought; he was handsome enough to be appealing and far more intelligent than anyone else his age that she knew of. If all she would ever have would be these few moments of him she thought, then memories of them would be more than fond.

In a way, she didn't want this to end; but when she saw her father and his eyes beginning to turn angry and protective, she knew the moment was indeed at its end.

Still, she felt she couldn't resist one last flirt. She turned around expecting to find him close behind her as he had been. He wasn't there. Instead he was standing on the very edge of the campsite looking in with his own delightful smile.

"Is this land too hostile for you pursue this conversation?" She teased.

"Like the ambitions of my father, Bors the Elder end at the border of his beloved friend Leon de Gras," he said bowing slightly in the direction of the great Knight, "So too does my aspiration to follow you end at this point out of sincere respect for yourself, your honor and the most honest respect for your father who has been such a good friend to mine."

The girl looked to her father whom she saw nod approvingly.

"Now if I may have your leave and the leave of his Lordship," Arthur said with another bow; "I must return to my own borders."

"My leave is granted," Leon de Gras answered and then the clever boy turned and walked away.

"I thought I asked you not to leave the campsite without an escort?" Leon de Gras asked his daughter.

"I'm not a little girl anymore, father. I can take care of myself."

"I can tell. That was made clear by you letting a young man whom you've never met before follow you back to camp. You're lucky that particular boy was honorable."

"How could I possibly be in any danger in a place filled to the brim with brave Knights with deadly weapons?" She asked in a voice with a touch of sharpness.

"Guinevere," her father said to her gently. "Not all Knights are deserving of their title and privileges. If you remember nothing else during the next three days, please remember that."

Arthur returned to the place he had left Betivere and Gawain and found them both greeting him with sly grins.

"Well...?"" Betivere pressed.

Arthur only smiled back and told them, "She gave great conversation."

They all laughed until Arthur told Gawain, "So now that you're a Knight, I suppose you're not on for tonight."

"What do you mean, 'not on'?" Gawain said as if insulted.

"Well, a respectable man like yourself surely can't be involved in such nefarious plans as we have."

"Surely not," added Betivere. "It might threaten his reputation that he has yet to develop."

"Oh I'm in alright," Gawain insisted. "You just try and keep me out."

That night, as the tavern tent first opened for business, three young men wearing masks entered the tent crowded with men all at one stage or another of drunkenness.

As the three of them stood in the entrance and having the full attention of every man therein, one of the boys said loudly, "Excuse me...can anyone tell me where I can find real men?" He then sniffed the air and stated, "It smells too much like cowardice in here."

Within seconds, fists, cups, flagons, showers of beer and ale and eventually the odd body or two were flying in all directions. For the third year in a row, the "Tavern Tent Brawl" proved a rousing success.

Lord Uriants

There were about thirty battered and bruised men left in the tavern after the brawl had been put down by Lord Uriants and his soldiers. They were all on their knees with their hands behind their heads and sharp, steel spearheads at their throats. Meanwhile Lord Uriants, the Duke of Westphalia slowly walked through them emphasizing his displeasure by making a point to scowl at each one.

"For the third year in a row," he lectured them in a voice like an animal's growl, "I have had to bring my soldiers into this tent when they are supposed to be keeping this entire site safe. And for what? A bunch of drunken buffoons who seem to think that acting like animals in the wild is somehow entertaining!"

As he continued his lecture, both Arthur and Gawain looked about the tent for Betivere, but he was nowhere to be found. "That would be typical of Betivere," Gawain thought to himself. "Let them start the trouble and then quickly duck out before getting caught."

"Three years in a row!" Uriants thundered. "Have you all forgotten the reason we are all here?"

Arthur was thinking roughly the same thing as well; except in a different tone. If Betivere had managed to escape before being caught then that was all the better for him. He could tell at a glance that Gawain was not so generous. The righteous beating of Betivere was likely the first thing on his agenda for if Lord Uriants let them live.

"Three years in a row! What am I to think about that? What am I to call it?"

"A tradition?" Arthur blurted out.

A highly unamused Uriants slowly approached the young man on the floor. His green eyes seemed ablaze with anger and the scowl on his chiseled face seemed to make his beard appear a deeper red.

"Was that supposed to be some kind of joke?" He growled at the young lad kneeling before him.

"A weak attempt to be sure," Arthur responded, "But I had hoped it would lighten the mood."

Uriants wasn't sure whether to slap this boy across the face or buy him a beer for being so bold. The number of people he could remember who had the courage to speak to him like that could be counted on one hand and all of those were Knights. This was a mere squire.

"May I speak frankly, My Lord?" Arthur asked.

"Will this be another feeble attempt at humor?"

"No, My Lord. I believe I've already learned a harsh lesson about that."

"Not harsh enough my standards you haven't. But as you have my undivided attention, I am now quite curious as to what you may have to say."

"Well..." Arthur began, but Uriants interrupted him.

"And if you're going to talk to me like a man, then stand up like one."

Arthur slowly stood up as to not alarm the soldier pointing a spearhead at his throat.

"Keep your hands where I can see them," Uriants reminded Arthur.

"As you well know," Arthur started, "For the first fourteen years of this competition, there was at least one fatality resulting from combat. The Knight who dealt the fatal blow would invariably be accused of murder and all those such accused were put to death."

"I'm well aware of this. Get to your point."

Well," Arthur coughed, "In the past three years there have been no fatalities. While there have been some rather gruesome injuries, not one contestant has died as a result."

"What has this got to do with grown men acting like idiots?"

"As Your Lordship is very well aware, before the first day of competition, there is a lot of excitement and anticipation. The Knights all know they will soon be going into combat and I'm sure the expectation of it only builds with each minute that passes from the time they arrive and the time the first blow is struck either by or for them."

Though still angry, Lord Uriants would have to confess that the boy was making sense.

"The brawl, while admittedly childish and a rather expensive waste of beer as a result, I feel serves as a kind of release for the brave men about to fight one another. It relaxes them and in a strange way helps to instill a sense of comradery in as much as it becomes a shared experience."

"So you're saying this is a good thing?" Uriants prodded.

"I wouldn't say 'good' per say; but definitely not evil."

"I see," Uriants said preparing to spring an intellectual trap on the young man, "So next year, we should just let this happen and not do anything about it."

"I'm hoping that a King is chosen this year, eliminating the need for this tournament all together."

Now Uriants was sincerely impressed. Not only had the boy given him something to think about, the lad had also managed to not step into the trap.

There was something more about this young man that Uriants detected. He was confident and self-assured. Most young men that he'd spoken to had practically soiled themselves (and a few literally) when the powerful Lord questioned them. Here in front of him was uncommon courage.

He also looked familiar, but he couldn't think exactly of whom the boy reminded him.

"I still think this is childish and wasteful," He told Arthur making sure to still sound angry. "But I have to confess you make an interesting, though not particularly convincing point."

"Thank you, My Lord."

"I've done nothing for you to thank me for, boy."

The expression on his harsh face then softened a little.

"How old are you?" He asked Arthur in a softer growl.

"Seventeen, My Lord."

"According to the rules we traditionally abide by during this tournament, you're too young by one year...however" he said trying to sound magnanimous, "I think we can bend them a little just this once."

He then shouted to the man behind the makeshift bar, "Get this young man a beer. And the rest of you may stay one more hour. If there is so much as one man passed out drunk after this hour, I will personally burn this tent down the ground."

He turned to leave but then turned back to face Arthur.

"You didn't happen to start this, did you?"

Arthur remembered that Uriants was rumored to be able to literally smell a lie, but still attempted a clever answer.

"I have to confess that I was contributing factor."

Once more, Uriants found himself impressed by the young man who had once again failed to fall into a trap.

"I trust you won't be contributing to any further nonsense?"

"I shall do my part to maintain peace in these proceedings."

Lord Uriants made a sound like a horse grunting, turned and left. After that Arthur breathed a sigh of relief feeling as he'd been found not guilty of a crime.

The Lake of Crystal Water

Later, Arthur and Gawain were walking on the torch-lit path leading back to the campsites. Gawain had just finished saying, "I'm going to poke what's left of eyes out and then skull..." when both he and Arthur spotted Betivere leaning against his staff and waiting for them.

"There you are, you goat!" Gawain called out. "I have half a mind to split you in two. Where did you go?"

"Evidently you didn't hear me yell, 'let's' get out of here, the Duke is coming' did you?"

"At whatever moment you chose to warn of us that, I was probably distracted by a man so drunk, he was trying to bite through my chain mail."

Holding up his arm, he noticed a disembodied tooth still stuck to the mail.

"You see this?" He asked angrily. "What in the world am I supposed to do with another man's tooth?"

"I've heard some people make rather fine necklaces out of them," Betivere answered.

"Is that what your friendship is really like? Is this is what I can expect if we're ever on the same battlefield?"

"Oh for the Lady's sake, you know I won't be like that!"

"Oh yes; you provided such a fine example of your loyalty tonight, didn't you?"

"Oh really? Who's idea was it to turn the latrine upside down five years ago? Compare that to who eventually admitting to being at fault."

"That was different."

"Lord Uriants wanted me flogged. Fortunately, I was saved by the fact that Uriants still owed my father money at the time."

"What a man has done five years ago can be completely undone by what he fails to do within a day," Gawain said as if reciting from a book.

"Oh my Great Lady! When did you learn to read?"

Gawain started to pull his dagger, but Arthur stepped in between them.

"Oh for heaven's sake!" He growled at them. "Nobody got hurt and no one will be tied to a stake and stripped naked tomorrow while raw vegetables are thrown at him!"

"Only because you managed to pull one over on Lord Uriants," Gawain said, his demeanor suddenly changed.

"Oh yes," Betivere agreed. "I heard your little speech. Even I was impressed. Uriants isn't known for being reasonable when he has to use his troops to put down a brawl."

"Don't try to change the subject, Betivere. Arthur might not have had to do that…"

"If we'd never started the fight in the first place," Arthur interrupted.

He then put his arms around the shoulders of his friends; partially to keep his balance. He'd managed to manipulate an additional pint of beer out of the bartender.

"Now look," he told them both, "It's getting late, we have to get up early in the morning…at least I do and we all know that if we don't go back to our sites soon, we're likely to get into further mischief. "

"You do have a point," Gawain said with resignation.

"Let's go back to our own camps, try to get some sleep and pray our parents never learn of what we just got away with."

"I think that's a good idea," Betivere agreed.

Gawain pointed at Betivere and told him with an angry scowl, "You still owe me."

Arthur decided that instead of taking the lit path back to the campsite, he would practice some of what Betivere had taught him about walking in the dark. It was a clear and cool summer night and the moon was half full making the venture a bit of a challenge, but not quite total darkness.

Along the way, he beheld a stunning site. The moon was hovering just above the horizon and its reflection on the water was like a silver road leading straight to its enigmatic face.

He couldn't help but be held almost in a trance watching the silvery light dance on the ripples in the lake and found himself feeling poetic at such a wonder before him.

"What wonders have you seen?" He said, staring straight at the half moon. "Did you see the first two lovers playing like children in the garden? Were you a witness to their fall from grace? Have you guided the spirits of the forest and water to distant lands and shores? Where were you when the world was new? Have you always been here? Or do the tales of Morgan and Bridgette speak truly? Are you truly the heart of love and the worker of its magic?"

At that moment, another dazzling sight appeared before him. A form appeared in the silver ripples, coming up from beneath the surface. The form was unmistakably that of the curves of a woman with her back turned to him.

Half submerged in the water and half in the open, he felt that her true beauty, that of her natural form without the false pretense of the costumes all men and women wear was shining through. Here she was the way that either the One God or the many had made her. It didn't matter. Here was a miracle all faiths could believe in.

She didn't see him when she turned and waded out of the lake and onto the shore. He could only see her silhouette and so didn't feel dirty or guilty at beholding her.

She dried herself with either cloth or fur and each movement was full of natural grace. He felt his heart quicken, but he was still able to temper the passion of his heart with the cool water of reason. It was only the outline of her body that he perceived, which stirred a fire within him. But to truly love her, he would have to know what was inside the form. He would have to know her soul.

Still, the sights he'd seen were more than worthy of remembering. He closed his eyes and silently prayed that this vision would never be forgotten even when the fire of youth had faded.

He was just about to turn and leave when he heard a harsh and drunken voice call out to the beautiful silhouette.

"Hello my love," the voice slurred. "Taking a bath are you?

Arthur looked to the source of the voice and saw a man stumbling towards her. She quickly covered herself as best as she could and challenged him.

"Who are you? " She demanded. "What do you want?"

The voice was unmistakably that of the beautiful girl he'd followed earlier that day and the thought of her in danger stirred another fire inside of him.

Feeling naked and vulnerable, Guinevere started backing away from the dark form coming toward her. She had hoped that her bath wouldn't be noticed and felt she'd nearly accomplished this. But here was a man coming at her and his drunkenness made him unpredictable.

She feared what he wanted with her and suddenly wished she hadn't come down to the lake at all.

"Now come on, love," he hissed like a snake, "Don't be shy. I'm not going to hurt you."

She frantically looked around for an escape route or a weapon to fight with; but it was too dark for her to see anything but the lake. She thought of diving back into the water to escape him, but he had cut her off from that possibility.

"Mind a little company, my pretty?"

"Keep away!" He snapped at him trying to sound brave. "Don't come near me!"

"Oh you don't mean that," the shadowy form as he came closer. "I think you came out here for a reason. I think you want some company tonight."

"My father is the Earl of Blackpool! He will kill you if you touch me."

"Oh I'm going to do far more than touch you my love. I'm going to touch you in places and in ways you've never dreamed."

She tried backing away again. Her courage spent, she heard herself begging.

"Please...go away!"

"I'll go away. I promise," he spat. "First I'm going to take what the night has given me."

She tried to run, but tripped over something hard. He felt his rough hands on her legs and he started to pull her over the ground. She screamed for help, hoping that there would be someone to hear her; but instead, only felt his fist strike her hard on her face.

"No use crying for help, my love," he told her as he turned her over. "Don't worry. It'll all be over soon."

Suddenly, she heard a thud close to her and the man tumbled to the ground.

Arthur had hit him with the first thing he could find, but it was clear he hadn't injured him enough. He still had the advantage, though. Now was the time to put Betivere's lessons to the test.

The man tried to get up, but when he got to his knees, someone he couldn't see kicked him hard in the gut, knocking him back down to the ground. As the man doubled over, Arthur quickly scrambled to the opposite side of where he'd just hit him.

The most important thing in fighting in the dark is to keep moving, Betivere had taught him. The unknown man tried raising himself again and Arthur sent him back to the ground with another kick.

He knew that he'd eventually have to kick him in the head to knock him out, but Arthur also knew that such a blow might kill him. Even if defending the honor of a lady, he might still die for murder. He had to maintain reason over his anger and stay focused.

"Where are you, you coward?" The drunken man demanded.

"Here," Arthur said as he hit him in the gut again with the tree branch.

The man fell again and had more trouble in his attempt to regain his feet. That same moment, Guinevere recognized the voice, but wasn't sure from where. She was too frightened and excited to think clearly.

As the man tried again to raise himself, his legs opened a little and Arthur saw an opportunity to strike his most vulnerable target. Even in the dark, he was able to nail the man in between the legs and when he fell and rolled over, Arthur knew he was ready for the final blow. He kicked him across the face and then the man rolled over and went limp.

Arthur was concerned that he might have accidentally killed the offender, but he could clearly hear him breathing. He saw the man try once more to move, but with a final groan, he went silent. Arthur could still hear him breathe and could see his chest rising and falling.

Arthur then looked around for the girl and at first didn't see her. Eventually, he saw her silhouette curled into a ball on the ground close to the water's edge. He started to walk toward her, but she must have heard his footsteps.

"Go away!" She snapped in a voice full of tears. "Don't come near me!"

He briefly thought of trying to calm her some way, but remembered his mother once telling him that it was complete foolishness for a man to try and calm an excited woman. The only thing to do was to be patient and let her calm on her own.

Still, he positioned himself between her and her attacker. Although fairly sure the brute would be unconscious probably until morning, he wasn't taking any chances.

Looking around, he saw what looked like some cloth near the water. When he went to it and picked it up, it was clearly a woman's dress. Hearing her sobbing, he approached her slowly and then placed the dress over her trembling body as if to cover her.

She jumped a little at the touch of the fabric, but as she was starting to settle down, she realized what it was. She tried to choke back her tears and somehow managed to order him, "Don't look at me."

"I assure you, I'm not," Arthur replied.

His own heart was pounding in his chest and he was starting to feel a ferocious headache coming on. The attacker was still lying on the ground, but he could hear that he was still breathing. In fact, the man had started to snore.

"Don't turn around," she told Arthur as he she slowly and shakily pulled the dress over her.

Having finished the labor of dressing, she suddenly found she couldn't move. She was standing, but her body seemed to want to fall. Anger, fear and humiliation all boiled inside of her and all she wanted to do was cry.

"I'm not a little girl anymore," she thought she said silently.

"You're not fully a woman either," the familiar voice told her, obviously trying to be gentle.

She suddenly felt a rage come over like she'd never known before. She lunged at the familiar voice and focusing all of her emotions on him, started striking him as hard as she could. After several blows, she felt him grab her wrists and turn her around.

She nearly panicked as she thought that the still unknown voice had become her assailant. But for what seemed like hours, he merely held her gently but firmly. At some point, she heard him say, "It's alright now. It's alright. You're safe."

Her pain and anguish finally took control of her and she began wailing like a child. While she did so for a time she wasn't sure of, he simply held her in his arms, letting her cry.

Guinevere

Guinevere could feel the swelling on her cheek where the attacker had struck her. Not only did it ache and throb, it was started to push against her left eye causing it to tear. Fortunately, the young man escorting her down the torch-lit path to her father's campsite couldn't see her face. Even if he did, he was being courteous enough not to say anything about it.

Arthur intentionally followed about five feet behind her and hadn't said a word since leaving the lake. He was fairly certain she wasn't going to want any man too close to her for the moment and his mother had once told him, "The absolute worst thing a man can say to an upset woman is anything at all."

Guinevere was shaking all over and even though it was late-spring, she felt cold. She was able to think though, which both aided and harmed her general state of mind.

"Stupid, stupid girl," She thought she said to herself. "Running and then begging for help like a child; just like a typical girl."

Unfortunately, at that moment Arthur forgot his mother's advice.

"That's probably because you are a girl," He told her.

She stopped and spun around, revealing angry eyes that seemed to be on fire. Arthur had never been afraid of any man, but this was the face of a creature more frightening than any he'd encountered.

Guinevere wanted to punch him squarely in the jaw, but stopped just short. Apparently the young lad knew he'd made a horrible mistake and his apparent fear of her made her feel less vulnerable.

"Was I really saying that out loud?" She asked.

"I'm afraid you were," the young man answered.

She regained her sense of calm and almost turned around to continue walking.

"I think it's best that we part ways at this point," She told the boy quietly.

"I'm not sure it's a good idea for you to be alone before reaching your campsite," Arthur replied.

"Of course you wouldn't…you're a man."

"I don't think that's quite…"

"Let me try and explain why it's a very bad idea that you follow me any further. First of all, I snuck out in the first place and seeing me come back with a boy in tow is not likely to be well-received by my very overprotective father."

"I can see that."

"Second, and this may be the most important reason, as soon as he sees this," she said pointing at the bulge on her face," He's going to want the head of the first man he sees. Out of appreciation for your help, I'd prefer that not to be you."

"That is also a very good point."

She then looked down at the ground feeling ashamed and vulnerable.

"I'm afraid I have nothing of my own that I can give you as reward."

A rather bawdy joke did come to Arthur's mind, but he thought better than to actually say it in this moment.

"That's where you're wrong," He told her gently. "There is something you can give me that I will cherish forever."

"What's that?" She asked him suspiciously.

"Your name."

"My name? Is that all?" She said with a chuckle.

There was that bad joke again.

"It's more than I'll likely ever have of you after tonight."

She felt a little sad at these words; especially as she knew he was most likely right. Whoever this young man was, in only a few short hours, she'd grown to like his wit, his courtesy, his humor and his gentle demeanor at just the right moment.

"I will gladly give it," She told him. "But only in exchange for yours."

With a slight bow and a gentle smile, he told her "My name is Arthur."

"And I am Guinevere."

They stood and stared at each other, neither one of them wanting this moment to end. It was Arthur who would decide it was time to part ways, no matter how much it would hurt.

"Then I bid you goodnight," he told her with another bow.

"To you as well."

Even though they had just said their farewells, they stood and stared at each other for another precious moment. Guinevere then decided that this exchange was getting a little silly.

"Right," she said suddenly. "Goodnight."

She started to leave him, but couldn't make herself turn around. She almost stumbled as she walked backward. At that moment, it was more important to keep looking at this wonderful young man than see where she was going. After another moment, she did turn and walk away, not knowing that Arthur hated this goodbye as much as she did; perhaps even more.

"Where the blazes have you been?" Were the first words her father said when Guinevere stepped into the campsite. This was actually less than she was expecting as he was still seated and didn't scream at the top of his lungs. That came just a moment later, when Leon de Gras noticed the huge lump on her face. His eyes then seethed with a hateful rage that Guinevere could swear she could actually feel.

"Father, I need you to try and calm down," She tried.

The attempt failed.

"Who did this to you? Where is the villain?"

"Father...please...I need you to relax."

"It was that boy I saw you with earlier today wasn't it?" he growled. "On your mother's soul I'll hack him to pieces!"

He stormed away and into his tent. Guinevere knew all too well what he was looking for.

"Father no!" She shouted angrily.

He spun around and his eyes had the look of insanity and disbelief at the same time.

"What do you mean, 'No'? It's a father's responsibility to protect his children."

"Yes father; I know that, but will you please just listen to me a moment before you go off and hack off the wrong head."

That, at least appeared to work. He stopped his frenetic looking about, stood still for a moment and glared at his beloved child. Guinevere knew she'd finally gotten through to him when he grunted, "Fine" and sat back down on his stoop.

Leon de Gras had been trying to protect his only daughter from the harsh reality of the world outside their castle for seventeen years. Among the many things that angered him at that precise moment was the thought that he'd finally given in to his knowledge that he couldn't keep her locked up like a prisoner forever.

She needed to see the world outside and be part of its life. She needed to experience both the good and evils of this world in order to better live within it. And now, the first time he lets her out of the cage, she gets assaulted...possibly worse.

Guinevere told her story as best as she could without breaking down. Telling the story felt almost like reliving it again; as if it were actually happening again. It took all of her strength, but she did manage to tell him all of it; even of the brave young man who came to her rescue.

After she was done, she could no longer manage the strength to hold back her emotions and as her father held her in his arms like he always had, she broke into tears again.

For his part, he felt he had done the best as he could considering the circumstances. Her mother had died when Guinevere was very little, making him the only parent she'd ever known.

He had considerable help from a female governess he'd hired years ago, but she died just when the little girl started to change into a woman. In this, the great Knight considered himself completely inadequate.

When she had emptied her tears, he pushed her gently away like he'd always done when leaving for any reason.

"Where are you going at this hour?" She asked him, still sniffling.

"I need to find your attacker and bring him to justice."

"You're not going to kill him are you?"

"This man needs to suffer for what he's done."

"But not by death. He may have scared me half to death, but not much more than that."

"He might have harmed you further if that young man of yours hadn't come along."

"Perhaps yes, but he still didn't actually rape me."

Her last words stung like that of a bee as he didn't even want to speak or hear the word, "Rape."

"For God's sake he tried to!"

"Intending to commit a crime and actually committing a crime are two different things, father. Does that sound familiar?"

He wanted to scream and shout at her to make her understand that she was wrong. Unfortunately, he knew that she wasn't.

"Yes," he said with a deep sigh, "And you cannot punish a man for a crime he has not actually committed."

"Exactly!"

After a few silent moments, she said something that nearly had him flying into a rage again.

"I will not be responsible for any man's death."

"In no way was any of this your fault," he told her sternly.

"Isn't it?" She pleaded. "If I hadn't have been out there..."

"It might have been someone else's daughter."

"But he was drunk! He lost control!"

"Neither of those are an adequate excuse. He's committed a crime. He needs to pay his due."

"But father, you can't. You can't be objective enough to judge this fairly."

His almost lost control again but managed to regain his senses quickly.

"In that, you are absolutely right," He told her. "This is why I'm going to speak to Lord Uriants."

"You mean 'King in all but name' Uriants?" She asked with a hiss in her voice.

She disliked Uriants; thinking him arrogant and self-righteous.

"I'm well aware of your opinion of Lord Uriants," Leon told his daughter. She was surprised by this as it was almost as if he could read her mind.

"And yes, he's a pompous, arrogant ass. He is, however very knowledgeable of the law and quite fair."

"You don't actually believe that nonsense that he can smell a lie, do you?"

"I generally don't care if it is or not," Leon said just before leaving. "In this case however, I'm rather hoping that it is."

King in all but Name

Lord Uriants listened to Leon des Gras' story of his daughter's assault with keen interest. In the history of the tournament and in particular his own life over the past seventeen years, there had been more than a few such incidents and no matter what measures were taken to prevent crime during the three-day event; almost invariably something was stolen, something caught fire and someone was hurt.

It usually fell on Uriants to police and judge these matters as he was the richest, most powerful of all the nobles competing for the crown.

He had the largest tracts of land in his domain in all the Land and unlike all the other Knights, Dukes and Earls of the Land, his wealth allowed him to maintain a standing army.

Only a few of the nobility could call up an entire army and then only for the summer months. At the end of the summer, the farmers and villagers conscripted had to return for the autumn harvest season. Uriants, however maintained his army throughout the year as he was able to pay his troops enough to remain in the army.

With this army came political power none of the others could dream of and it almost always fell on Uriants to adjudicate criminal activity during the tournament.

But this incident was different. The man reporting the assault was an old friend; one Uriants had known since childhood and fought alongside in numerous campaigns.

They had even fought in the Great Battle in which Uther Pendragon was chosen to receive Excalibur and become King. He was having great difficulty maintaining control over a temper that had become legendary knowing this friend had been injured.

In addition, the child Guinevere was one he'd seen grow from infancy. He had been there for his friend at the birth of his children just as Leon des Gras was there for the birth of his son. And just as Leon had comforted him after the death of his own beloved son, Uriants was also there to help ease the pain of his friend when his adored wife died in childbirth. Hearing of Guinevere's assault felt almost as if he was listening to a report of an attack on his own child.

The more emotional Leon des Gras was in reporting the attack, the more difficulty Uriants had in maintain the ability to judge the matter objectively. When Leon's voice cracked, Uriants nearly wept as well.

"You're not going to want to hear this," Uriants told his friend, "But it has to be said. Your daughter is right. I cannot punish a man for a crime for which he did not commit."

"What do you mean 'did not commit?'" Leon asked angrily. "My daughter's face is so swollen, she's barely recognizable."

"I was referring to her being raped," Uriants said. "I'm assuming you wished the assailant charged with rape, is that not true?"

"You know me better than that," Leon said dramatically. "If it were anyone else's child, I would have no difficulty judging this matter on the stricture of the law."

"But it is your child. And that, I was afraid may have clouded your judgment. I'm pleased to see that I was mistaken."

"That's the reason I came to you, instead of rectifying it myself."

"A wise decision, my friend; and not one that I can guarantee I would have made myself had it been my child."

Leon chuckled a little as he still struggled to hold back tears.

"You might have wanted the man drawn and quartered," Leon attempted to joke.

"Ten years ago, I would have carved him open myself."

To this, they both laughed. Uriants then placed his hand on Leon's shoulder in an almost brotherly way.

"I'm sure the girl is in good hands," Uriants told his old friend. "But will you be alright?"

"I need to know what you're going to do," Leon answered.

"Well, the first thing I have to do is find these two men your daughter spoke of."

Leon felt a little confused and tried to remind Uriants that Guinevere had only spoke of one assailant.

"I'm also referring to the young man who defended her honor," Uriants replied. "I'd like to think that any man would have done what he did, but we both know that isn't the case. I need to reward him publicly so as to encourage others to be so brave in the defense of the innocent. While someone's motivation may be greed or attention, the proverbial 'Right thing to do' still gets done."

"I heartily agree."

Uriants saw his friend back to his own campsite and left him there. He'd hoped he could get a glimpse of Guinevere to see the damage with his own eyes, but he did not. She was safely tucked away in her tent with two of Leon des Gras' sons standing guard.

More than one hope went in and out of Uriants' mind as he, along with ten of his soldiers made their way down to the Lake. The first was the obvious hope that the man was still passed out and that the he was the only man passed out on the lake's shore. To his own frustration, he also found himself hoping that the culprit either was or was not one of his own soldiers or Knights as both would be problematic. If it turned out to be someone else's vassal or soldier, he'd have a more complicated task in punishing him. If the man was one of his own, he would have no difficulty at all; however, what would be the effect on his own men's morale seeing there commander punishing one of his own men?

At this, he reminded himself that it would ultimately be necessary, no matter how upset his Knights and troops might become.

They had to know that he would not just let them get away with anything and they needed just enough fear of him to respect the consequences of criminal action.

To Uriants' relief, he found that there indeed was a man passed out by the Lake and he was alone. However, when the torch was lifted over the man's face to reveal it, Uriants' heart dropped and his blood began to boil. The man was not only known to him; but was none other than his own youngest brother, Sir Fulton of Whitehall.

Not a Delicate Flower

Arthur was almost asleep, making it even more annoying to being roused than if he'd actually been sleeping. It was that soft, pleasant feeling of having finally found a comfortable position and drifting off that is one of the more pleasing sensations to a young man who spent most of his days working on a farm.

He had told his father of the previous fight he'd had with the unknown man and his father had woken him by telling him that Lord Uriants was looking for the young man who had defended the honor of the young lady. Although slightly suspicious of Uriants' reasons, he knew that avoiding this summons would only prove to be worse than whatever awaited him.

Still rubbing his tired eyes, he followed his father down the torch lit path to what had been the tavern tent; now converted into a makeshift court.

"No matter what Lord Uriants asks you," his father reminded Arthur, "Be absolutely truthful. The man can smell a lie."

"Is that really true?" Arthur asked.

"Unless you want to be flogged in the morning, you'd better assume that it is."

Outside the tent, Bors the Elder reminded Arthur that it would be better if Arthur followed him inside and to stay behind him out of sight until called upon.

"If he does call for you," The older Knight told his son, "Step forward, announce yourself and then don't say another word until he speaks to you. If he asks you questions, answer them as directly, but briefly as you can. Do not add any information that isn't necessary."

"You act like I'm the one on trial," Arthur joked.

"Once he finds out you're not a Knight, you may be."

"There's no law that says…"

"Just do what I tell you to and don't argue with me. And unless you have to have a pound of your flesh ripped off of your back, don't even think of arguing with him."

Inside the tent, Arthur saw the almost comical sight of a man kneeling on the ground with two of Uriants' soldiers holding spears to his throat. To Arthur's slight dismay, the man was wearing the unmistakable tunic of a Knight. And it wasn't just any tunic. He wore the Scarlet Dragon of Westphalia.

He was also wearing a very noticeable bruise on the right side of his face where Arthur had kicked him.

Arthur also noticed Guinevere standing next to her father. Even with the swelling on her face, she was still the most beautiful face in the room; which wasn't too difficult as she was the only woman.

His heart beat a little faster when she apparently noticed him. Her eyes began to sparkle, a smile began to cross her face but she restrained it and her cheeks reddened with blush.

Lord Uriants then stepped forward as he was clearly the man who would be judging the proceedings.

"Are we all here?" He asked impatiently.

The other Knights and Lords assembled in the tent murmured that they were.

"Very well," he continued. "Will the accuser step forward?" Guinevere stepped forward with her father still by her side.

"Will you please state as briefly as possible what happened earlier tonight that your father has asked me to adjudicate?"

With much more courage and confidence than most men were used to from women, Guinevere briefly told her story.

"Not more than two hours ago," She began, "I was bathing in the lake. After I was finished, a man approached me and assaulted me. During the assault, he punched me in the face and dragged me across the ground. It was then that a brave young man defended my honor by attacking and subduing my assailant."

Lord Uriants was slightly startled by her telling of the story. He expected tears and sniveling; not this example of courage and strength.

"That's...very direct and to the point," He said to Guinevere.

There was no fear in her eyes and she clearly wasn't lying. Had the evidence not been before his very eyes, he might have thought a man were standing in front of him. This was obviously the daughter of Leon des Gras.

"That man who attacked you," he asked her, "Do you see him here?"

"I do indeed," She said confidently.

"And where is he?"

"He's kneeling in between the rather surly looking soldiers with spears."

Several of the spectators started laughing, but Uriants quickly silenced them.

"This is no time for laughing!" He shouted. He then turned to the young woman and told her, "I'll thank you not to embellish your story with any more attempts at humor."

She thought of several spicy things to say in response, but thought better of it. Uriants glared at her and she returned his fiery gaze for a moment, but then decided that it would be better if she acted like a typical woman just for the moment. She looked away and let Uriants think he'd won that contest.

"It wasn't me," the man on the ground protested. "I swear it...it wasn't me."

The stench of the lie and the pathetic nature of his own brother's pleas turned Uriants' stomach. He felt like striking him across the face and nearly did; but he had to control his anger in order to be a fair judge. His brother's continued pleas of, "I would never hurt such a vision of loveliness..." did however deserve his sternest voice.

"Silence!" He shouted.

He then turned his attention back to the girl, hoping that perhaps a question phrased another way might give him hope of not having to punish his own flesh and blood.

"And you're absolutely sure this is the man?" He asked, hoping the girl would either be unsure or lie.

"I have no doubt," she answered confidently.

Unfortunately, there was no lie to be detected from her, only the foul odor of his brother's lies still spewing from his mouth.

"It wasn't me," he moaned, "I swear it. It wasn't me."

Guinevere's assailant then desperately turned to the girl and pleaded with her.

"I didn't mean you no harm; honest I didn't. I was only having a little laugh."

Leon des Gras, who had held his own temper back for longer than he'd wished stepped toward him and started to draw his sword.

"How dare you speak to my daughter, you filth!"

It took three other Knights to hold him back.

His heart breaking and his rage threatening to flash like lightning, Uriants searched for some relief from the pain of the decision he would have to make.

"And do you see the young man who saved you in this tent?" He asked Guinevere.

"I do indeed," She said with a smile.

"For the love of the One God, please point him out."

She pointed in the direction of the young man standing just visible behind Bors the Elder. As she did, Arthur stepped forward and silently bowed to Lord Uriants. To Arthur's surprise though, Uriants did not appear pleased.

His already angry eyes began to boil with rage and he gritted his teeth.

"Am I to understand that a man that is not a Knight assaulted a man of noble blood?" Uriants thundered.

At that moment, Arthur understood his father's earlier concern.

"Who are you?" Uriants shouted. "What right do you have to assault anyone above your station?"

Arthur was about to answer when his father stepped in front of him.

"He's my son," Bors said to Uriants like a challenge. "I may not be as highly ranked as you, but that does not make him a commoner."

"What is he then? A squire?"

"He is squire to myself and my elder son."

"So a lowly squire assaulted my brother! Is that it?"

"If your judgment is going to be tainted by your arrogant prejudice," Bors told Uriants, "Then I will protest these proceedings and demand a different judge; one who might not be so kind to your dear brother."

"You wouldn't dare..."

Another Knight stepped in between the two and as Arthur looked around, he saw half the men that all the men in the tent had their hands on their swords.

Uriants took a couple of deep breaths to try and calm himself after he backed away from Bors the Elder. He finally found a question that might help him save some face as he knew he'd obviously lost the argument.

"This entire plain is crawling with Knights," he screamed at Arthur. "Why didn't you try and find one?"

Arthur thought carefully for a moment before answering.

"I felt more immediate action was necessary at the time," he told the powerful Lord; though he could barely hide his sarcasm.

Uriants glared at Arthur with fiery eyes, but Arthur did not look away. The high ranking Knight then snorted like a horse and turned away. After a moment, he then spoke loud enough for everyone in the tent to hear.

"I need a moment alone with the accused!"

As the tent emptied out, Arthur was pulled aside by his father.

"That sharp tongue is going to get your head sliced off one of these days," Bors told him.

"I thought I showed great restraint over my wit with that answer."

"Yes and you're lucky Uriants isn't twenty years younger. He'd have skewered you like a boar."

Just like a typical teenager, Arthur rolled his eyes at his father's warning. Out of the corner of his eye, he noticed Guinevere being escorted by her father. She noticed him as well and this time didn't restrain a smile. His father punching him in the shoulder brought him back to reality.

"Are you listening to me?" He asked Arthur.

"Do I ever?"

Bors the Elder shook his head in frustration and out of the corner of his eye noticed the young Guinevere looking back at Arthur and beaming. He then placed his hand gently on Arthur's shoulder and told him, "On the other hand, there are far worse reasons to nearly be disemboweled by Uriants."

"Would you have risked the mighty Lord's wrath for such beauty?" Arthur asked.

"A thousand times in a day," Bors answered.

Back in the tent, Uriants waited until he was sure he was alone with his brother. When he was confident no one would hear him, he finally spoke.

"I can't let you get away with it this time," He told the younger man.

"Oh come on brother," he whined. "I've done worse."

"How dare you call me brother!" Uriants spat. "And **I know** you've done far worse. But this is no unknown country girl you imbecile. She's the daughter of a noble and a friend."

"Please brother...it won't happen again. I promise."

"How many times have I heard you swear that?"

"Just one more time. I'll never harm another woman again. I swear."

"I can fully assure you that this will be the last time. I'm going to make sure of it."

The following dawn, the entire temporary town was woken in order to witness the fulfillment of the sentence handed down by Lord Uriants. In a last attempt to spare his brother any misery, he passed down a sentence that on the surface seemed just: ten lashes with a bullwhip to be given by the victim.

However, there were many not satisfied with the sentence as it seemed obvious to them that a woman would never be able to inflict any serious pain or suffering on someone who had inflicted suffering on her. Already rumors of nepotism and unjust favoritism were floating through the camps. There was even consideration by some of inflicting their own proper justice after the mock punishment was performed.

The accused didn't help matters by laughing and joking about how a woman flogging him would be more like being "tickled" or a "massage." This reference infuriated Leon des Gras as it seemed to infer the "massage" of a prostitute and hearing his daughter referred to in such a manner caused his blood to boil.

The only person other than the accused that didn't seem unsettled, indeed pleased by the sentence was Guinevere who, with her assailant tied to a yoke and his back exposed seemed to be looking forward to the experience.

"Here comes the maiden to give me my massage," Uriants' brother sickly laughed. He even looked right at Leon des Gras and winked as he said, "I'll pay her extra if she gets the right spot."

Unfurling the whip, Guinevere smiled, scoffed and unfurled the long whip to its full length.

"Did you know I was raised on a farm?" She asked her assailant.

She then swung the whip high in the air and swirled it in order to make the tail go as fast as possible.

With a loud whistle, she brought the tail down on the naked back of the man who was now to be her victim. With a loud snap, the tail came down and buried itself in the flesh of the now disgraced Knight. With another strong movement, she made the tail drag through the flesh, taking a chunk of skin with it.

With a smile and a glint in her eye, she then told the screaming attacker, "That's one."

The First Day Part I:

An Unusual Invitation

After the public whipping had to be stopped when the Knight had passed out, the small town on the plain sprung into life as everyone prepared for the first day of the competition.

Spectators scrambled for open seats while guards of the higher ranking and more powerful Knights and Lords kept people out of the boxes reserved for their masters.

Venders, now hours behind schedule because of the whipping scrambled to prepare the food and drink they would sell during the competition. Knights and those who attended them darted back and forth around the grounds and the campsites.

All the while, the most accomplished pickpockets in the world robbed the unwary blind.

Arthur was helping his brother prepare for the tournament's first day by helping him with his armor of hardened leather plate. His brother was still a "growing boy" and the armor didn't fit quite as well as it had when first designed.

Bors the Younger wasn't helping matters with his constant whining about one plate being too tight or too much flesh being exposed on one side.

"This is supposed to be both protective and comfortable," the brother moaned.

"And it was made six months ago," Arthur answered. "You've added a little more girth since then."

"Well what am I supposed to do?" Bors the Younger complained. "I can't just shrink now can I?"

"You could lay off the pastries."

Meanwhile Bors the Elder watched with a mixture of pride and bemusement. Here his own flesh and blood would continue to keep the Knightly tradition of their family going; but he couldn't help but smile and barely withhold a laugh seeing the two boys bicker as they did. It reminded him of his own youth and his own beloved brother lost so long ago.

Just then a messenger wearing the black sash of a servant of Leon des Gras entered the campsite.

"May I have your permission to enter your campsite, My Lord?" The messenger asked politely.

"Of course," Bors the Elder answered cordially. "What news does my friend Leon des Gras have for me?"

"Begging your pardon My Lord, but this message is for your son, Arthur. Is he here?"

"I'm behind the monstrous mass of the brave, young Knight who's about to get his ass kicked," Arthur replied from somewhere behind Bors the Younger.

Bors the Elder called Arthur's name with a mildly warning tone just as Arthur stepped up to the messenger.

"Good morning," Arthur said politely.

"My gracious Lord Leon des Gras," The messenger told him, "Has asked me to extend an invitation to a brave and honorable young man to sit with him in his box for the first day of competition."

"Too bad there's no one here that meets that description," Bors the Younger spat out.

Arthur was surprised and confused. Was this gratitude? Was Leon des Gras going to give him some kind of reward? Perhaps even the lady's hand? He looked over at his father for some hint of guidance. In between puffs of his pipe, Bors the Elder told Arthur, "You shouldn't need my advice on this one. I would think the answer would be fairly obvious."

"I'll tell you what Arthur," the brother added, "Why don't you refuse and see what happens?"

Ignoring his brother's remark (which Arthur would later have to confess was very clever considering its source), he asked the messenger, "What time?"

"Competition begins in about an hour," Bors the Elder answered for the messenger, "I would think he wants you to arrive sometime before then."

"Is His Lordship in his box now?" Arthur asked.

"Not yet, but will arrive shortly," The messenger shortly answered.

"Then please inform His Lordship that I would be delighted and will join him as soon as I've finished stuffing my brother into his armor."

The messenger then bowed politely and then disappeared.

Arthur then turned to his brother and told him, "I think the stricture of the armor may be forcing more blood into your brain and making you more clever. I can't remember you saying two intelligent things in a row since...well...ever."

A little less than an hour later, Arthur jogged over to the stadium that the campsite surrounded. It sat on a rise in the shadow of the hill overlooking it. Designed almost in the form of a horseshoe, it was semi-circular with an opening at one end resembling where a section of a perfect circle had been cut out.

Feeling a little nervous, Arthur looked around the crowds at the stadium's entrance for some clue as to how he was actually going to find or get to Leon des Gras. He felt a little relieved by the sight of two Knights both wearing the black tunics of the House of des Gras.

The two Knights looked so much alike, Arthur thought that they surely must be twins. They even had the same scowl on their faces when they inspected Arthur.

"Excuse me sirs," Arthur addressed them politely.

Almost all of the men and most of the women at this annual event were of higher social rank than Arthur and he was constantly having to virtually bow and scrape before them. This was a fact of life that Arthur had mostly accepted, but often grated at him.

"I received a message..." Arthur continued but was interrupted.

"You Arthur?" One of the twins asked.

"That would be me, yes."

"Right…come on," the twin said to Arthur and with a motion of his head bade Arthur to follow him.

The structure of the stadium rose in twenty levels of wooden benches over a circular field of dirt. The grass that had once grown here had been torn up years previously and was not likely to grow again.

The very top level of the stadium were the boxes reserved for the highest ranking; a selective club of which Leon des Gras was a member. Overlooking the stadium and perched on top of a hill was a single, large bolder; buried deep within this rock was the sword Excalibur, waiting to be drawn by the one who would be King.

The two Knights led Arthur to the door behind the box. Entering the box, Arthur saw six more young men that looked almost alike, but that wasn't the most impressive part.

Instead of the hard benches of the stands under the boxes, the box was full of plush, velvet-lined couches and chairs (all black of course). There was a fully stocked bar at one end and what looked like a square window with a closed sliding wooden door. Just as Arthur was about to ask about the window, it slid open and four roast chickens appeared.

"It's about time!" One of the young men announced and they all rushed to the window.

"You hungry?" One of the twins asked Arthur.

"What happens if I say yes?"

"You get fed."

"In that case, I could use something to eat."

Just after that Arthur was presented with his own roast chicken and then found an empty seat, the door opened and everyone in the box quickly stood up. Knowing that this probably meant the arrival of his host, he stood as well.

The box had filled up more by the time Leon des Gras arrived. The merchants, clergy and town officials he was constantly working to keep happy all politely bowed, but the Knights knew that they didn't have to. Leon looked around the box briefly looking for the brave young man who had defended his daughter's honor and it didn't take long to find him.

Arthur showed the correct deference to Lord Leon and when he raised his eyes to look up at the Lord, he noticed Guinevere standing behind her father and smiling. He noticed too late that he was also holding the plate with the chicken and before he could turn to set it down, Leon took the plate away saying, "Thank you. That's very kind."

Arthur then started to move back to the out-of-the-way corner spot he'd found, but Leon des Gras stopped him.

"No, no, no," He told Arthur in his deep, booming voice. "You shall sit next to me and my daughter. That is the very least I can do to show my appreciation for you."

Lost in Guinevere's smile again, he felt almost as if floating as he maneuvered through the other spectators in the box to the seat next to Guinevere. As he sat, he heard the sound of furniture scraping across the wooden floor.

Without looking at Arthur, Leon des Gras told him, "Keep your hands where I can see them."

He looked behind him and saw that eight young Knights wearing black had moved closer to himself and Guinevere; all having decidedly unpleasant expressions in their eyes.

"Have you met my brothers?" Guinevere asked.

The stadium quickly filled with spectators creating a noise not unlike bees in their hives. The most junior Knights sat on long wooden benches around the field. Some had been in this competition before; but many had not. Their hearts pounded in their chests with feelings of both nervous anticipation and terror.

The Lords had taken great measures to make the competition as relatively safe as possible. They had eliminated the joust which resulted in horrific injuries and all too many fatalities. Now, only blunted swords could be used and even these could kill or maim.

Occasionally, there would be cheers from the crowd as a high ranking Lord like Uriants or Belvidere of Sunderland arrived in their boxes. But the spectators all knew that this was only a taste of pageantry before the real action. The best was yet to come.

Suddenly, a gust of wind blasted its way into the stadium and began to swirl in the center, like a tornado of dust. The crowds all began instantly cheering as they knew this sign could only mean one thing.

The trumpeters all blasted a loud and proud flourish as the tornado spun faster and higher. Suddenly doves all began flying from the tornado and then a shower of white rose petals.

"Now there's something we haven't seen before," Leon des Gras said impressed.

"Every year, he gets a little more complicated," Guinevere happily added.

Paper banners flew from the tornado and then small pastries and finally gold coins showered the stadium causing reactions from the crowd of excitement and appreciation.

A single flame then wrapped its way up the column of dust until it became a pillar of fire. The crowd roared in approval and then the pillar ascended and then disappeared into the brilliant blue sky.

A single figure in a black, hooded robe stood in the center of the field. As he pulled the hood of the robe slowly back, the ground cheered even louder. Merlin had arrived.

The First Day Part II:

Let the Festivities Begin

His hair was a brilliant snow white. His piercing eyes seemed to have both the energy of youth and the wisdom of extreme old age and he had a smile on his face that seemed to indicate a secret that only he would ever know. The heavy, black robe over his shoulders hid his body and his hands were hiding inside the oversized sleeves.

There was no mistaking that this was Merlin, the ancient sorcerer with a connection to the old gods of the forests and the streams.

This was the Merlin who had called forth all the strongest Knights and Lords to fight for an entire year on the plain of Surranam. This was the Merlin who had given the sword Excalibur to Uther Pendragon who ruled as King for less than a full year. And this was the Merlin who betrayed the Lady Igrain.

There were many who blamed him for the misfortunes that befell the Land and the people who represented it. There were also an equal number of those who believed that Merlin was the only hope of the Land's salvation.

Today, he was nothing more than a showman. His purpose in these events were to start the tournament and under no circumstances to interfere with its outcome. That had been his pledge so many years before and it was a word he had kept.

He had performed his magic trick of entering the arena that each year had become just a little more complex. And now he knew it was time to perform his other most important function of this gathering: reminding all of the rules that had been agreed upon over the course of nearly two decades.

As the crowd continued to cheer in appreciation, he raised one of his hands and the cheers fell silent.

"And so we have come together again," he said in a voice that though seemingly quiet, echoed off the stadium walls and the hills just beyond.

"Once more we have gathered together as a people for the purpose of witnessing the coming of a King. Once more all hearts and eyes look for one brave, strong and noble man to earn his right to climb the now sacred hill and try to draw the Sword of Kings from its prison in the stone. Once more we pray for a King to come to make the Land and the people one. And once more, our hopes and dreams for not only our own future, but the future of generations to come are cast out onto the brave men who have to compete for the chance to be chosen by whatever criteria the sword Excalibur demands and unite us all under one banner!"

Like an experienced actor or musician, Merlin waited for his applause to make its way through the crowds.

"But this is not an exercise in chaos," He continued. "This will not be a blind and bloodthirsty melee in which brothers and cousins may indiscriminately destroy one another. We have learned that once a King is chosen, he must have his vanquished foes as allies and friends on his side. Thus we have chosen to govern this tournament with rules designed to maintain the honesty of the crucible of battle; but leave no ill will between friends and families."

"The rules are thus: the joust has been forsaken in favor of the blunted sword. In this way, the skill and strength of the combatants is the true test and not merely a test of chance. Since favoring a contest of swords, fewer Knights and Lords have met either their end or a long life without their favorite body parts."

He allowed a moment for the crowd to laugh at his little joke and then continued.

"To begin the contest, the youngest, most junior ranked Knight will be brought forward and he may choose of any Knight waiting his turn on the bench. Whomever wins this first contest may then choose an opponent he desires. If a contestant loses on his first challenge, then I'm afraid his tournament is over. However, should a Knight win two contests in a row, he may come back for the second day of competition.

"If a Knight wins three contests in a row, then he has proven himself worthy. He may then ascend the hill and with the will of all that is sacred, he may attempt to draw the sword. Should he succeed, he is King! Should he fail however...then his tournament is also over."

"All who succeed in earning the second day of competition will then face one another with the same rules. Should there be a need for the third day of competition, then those who have not been eliminated will face one another in single elimination combat. The last man standing will climb the hill and confront his fate."

"Should a King come forth," Merlin said, his voice echoing even louder, "Then all the Knights and Lords must come forward and swear fealty to this one King who will rule the Land. Any who does not, immediately invites war and ruin onto his house, his lands and his people. However, should a King not come forward for another year, then we will simply return to this place and season another year to follow. That is the way it has been for sixteen years now..." He paused for dramatic effect, "Let us hope that this may be the last."

The crowds cheered, applauded and whistled their approval. Arthur was just as impressed as everyone else, but attempted to subdue his enthusiasm.

With nine men around him that all had the legal right to kill him for virtually any reason, he felt a low profile was the wisest approach to this situation.

Merlin raised his hand again and the crowd fell silent once more.

"Gawain of Cornwall," his voice bellowed. "I believe that you are the youngest and lowest ranking Knight this year. Will you please come forward?"

Gawain gathered his blunted sword and his helm and strode anxiously, but confidently into the center of the ring. He had preparing for this moment for many weeks and though it would likely shock those who would observe his actions, he knew that it was the best thing to do.

"Who will be your opponent, Sir Gawain?"

Gawain was almost too excited and nervous to say the name, but with a deep breath, he called out, "Sir Betivere of Sunderland."

A sudden gasp went through the crowd as Betivere was well known to be nearly blind. Despite this, he was a Knight and permitted to participate in the competition.

Many thought at the moment though that Gawain had purposefully chosen a lesser opponent just to earn an easy victory. But Gawain knew that this was not the case. As Betivere made his way into the center, guided by his cane only Gawain and Merlin knew that this would be no easy victory.

"Are you sure you want to embarrass yourself this early in the competition?" Betivere teased Gawain.

"I wanted to get my toughest competition out of the way first," Gawain replied with an excited growl in his voice.

"Remember gentlemen," Merlin whispered to them. "The first to find his way to the ground is the loser."

Merlin knew they were only half listening, but they knew the rules. He also knew why Gawain had done this. Neither one of them had much of a chance to earn the chance at the Sword.

Here were two young men wanting to put on a show either to make themselves more attractive to Knights or Lords who would want them in battle or to young ladies who might be able to sneak away from their parents after the first day's event.

The two young men made last second adjustments to their armor and helms and then Gawain raised his sword in a high guard. Betivere stood perpendicular to Gawain, shut his eyes and took a deep breath through his nose to clear all the senses he would need.

Before Merlin even finished saying, "You may begin" and with the roar of the crowd, Gawain's sword and Betivere's staff flew into action.

Betivere's staff was made of a black wood that was as hard and tough as steel. As the two men's weapons whirled and whistled through the air, when they crashed together, it made a loud and distinctive cracking sound like a hammer against a wooden plank.

All of the Knights observing, including the older and higher ranking were astounded by what they saw. Gawain and Betivere were moving so fast, it almost seemed as they were one unit.

Gawain's great strength made his heavy sword feel as light as a feather and Betivere's thin and light staff could be wielded with ease. They both spun and twirled with each swing, strike and blow; and so gracefully, it almost looked as if they were dancing.

Gawain had exceptional vision and could see so far out of the corner of his eyes, some claimed he could see behind him. Betivere could not only hear Gawain's sword whistling through the air, he could feel the air itself being moved by both his friend and the weapon he fought with.

Even Arthur, who had seen these two spar many times was impressed. At one point, the dust being kicked up by their furiously fast movements almost obscured them completely, but to the spectators' further astonishment, the battle went on and on far longer than many would have believed possible.

Surely one of them must tire, everyone thought. Surely one of them is human.

It would be Gawain that would make the fatal error. He overreached himself in a swing and instead of connecting with Betivere's staff, he found only empty air. Betivere then swept his staff under Gawain's feet and he fell to the ground.

At first, Gawain felt crushed. He had been looking forward to this competition for so long he couldn't honestly remember. He'd trained for years and had given his all in battle only to be defeated. It hurt more than any other wound he'd ever suffered.

But as Betivere helped him up, they were both surprised to hear the crowd roar in appreciation. Looking up and around into the stands, they saw that everyone was standing and shouting. Some were even throwing coins into the ring with them.

"Well done gentlemen," Merlin told him in his smooth, deep voice. "I suspect more than one maiden may sneak away from their parents tonight and find themselves in your company."

The two Knights embraced each other like brothers and with the crowd still roaring after him, Gawain marched proudly off of the field holding his head high almost as if he'd been victorious.

The First Day Part III:

A Victor Comes Forth

Betivere's next opponent, though not the challenge Gawain had been, proved to more difficult than he anticipated. Although he would be victorious, the victory would leave him almost exhausted. His arms and his legs burned and ached and his armor and helm felt as though their weight was crushing his shoulders.

His first victory had assured him a place in the second day. His second assured of the third day should one be necessary. But he knew there was little chance of a third victory in his condition. In order to not be too humiliated in defeat, he chose as his third opponent Galbreath of Merkos who was rumored to be a giant.

Sitting in the circle of benches surrounding the central field, Galbreath dwarfed even the tallest Knight sitting beside him. The wooden bench creaked in appreciation as he relieved it of its heavy burden and his footsteps were so heavy, they could be heard even in the highest boxes.

As the behemoth strode toward the awaiting Betivere, the young Knight came to fully understand how close he was to the ultimate goal of being King.

He'd never thought of it before. He'd never even dreamed of it. But at that moment, he became fully aware of the fact that if he could somehow pull off a victory against even this mountain of a man, he would next ascend to the top of the barren hill and if he could draw Excalibur from its resting place. For the first time in his life, he believed that he could be King.

It was an enticing, even exhilarating thought and he felt more strength start to well up inside of him. Could it be possible, he thought? As he felt the ground tremble slightly under his feet and felt Galbreath's cold shadow completely cover him, the delicious possibility all but disappeared.

Galbreath attempted the first blow, but missed badly. He swung wildly again, but once again Betivere easily dodged it.

In that instant, Betivere thought there might be a chance again and with blinding speed, hit Galbreath with a brilliant combination of blows to the back of the knees and Galbreath's enormous head. He didn't budge...not an inch.

Instead he swung his sword and although the staff was not broken, the force of the blow lifted Betivere into the air and slammed him to the ground.

In accordance to tradition, Galbreath reached down to help his fallen opponent to his feet. His huge hand closed completely around Betivere's and even his wrist as he picked up his victim as easily as a child picks up a doll made of rags.

"Are you injured?" Galbreath asked in his heavy, deep voice.

"Why no...not at all. Thank you for the experience."

Galbreath was defeated by Sir Tristan who jumped on his back and tickled him under the ribs. Unfortunately as Galbreath fell like a mighty tree, he took Tristan down with him and both were eliminated.

As such often happened, it was left to Merlin to choose another competitor and he chose Siegfried who was then defeated by Roy of Weisskatze.

Only one other Knight was able to defeat more than one opponent and that would be Bors the Younger. His defeat of Smithers of Burnes and then Bartholomew of Springfeld finished off the last of the lower-ranking Knights.

After his brother was defeated, Arthur straightened up in his chair as to give the message that it was time to leave. Before he could stand though, he felt a soft hand take hold of his. Looking, while not trying to obviously look, he saw that Guinevere had taken his hand and he was certainly not going to let the opportunity to hold hers pass him by.

Next came the Counts. The first of these, Count Floyd of Mellonviles easily dispatched the skilled but inexperienced Bors. There were, at that time a dozen or so Counts and not one of them managed to defeat more than one.

Count Orloff of Schreck was the last Count standing and the only opponents left to challenge were the Lords, Uriants Duke of Westphalia, Leon des Gras of Blackpool and Belvidere Earl of Sunderland.

Cornwall had already been represented by Gawain. And just as in all the years that previously passed; Drachenheim and the city of Camelot, the former home of Uther Pendragon still had no one claiming that Duchy.

The sun was hovering just over the western hills and the distant "Dragon Scale" mountains when Leon des Gras took his place on the battle field.

With him, a fearsome, but honorable reputation came with him. He was famed as one of the strongest warriors in all the Land and all of his years of experience had made him one of the most cunning.

Despite his skill and cunning, he had never ascended to the top of the hill. But today, he knew his chance had finally come. He had easily defeated Orloff before and in only three crossings of their swords, he defeated Orloff again.

Next came Belvidere of Sunderland. His fame was equal to the Earl of Blackpool, but he was older. He knew going into this years' competition that this was his last chance to raise the Sword. If he did not become King this time, it would fall on his son Betivere to win the crown in the name of Sunderland in years to follow.

This duel was only outdone by the contest between Gawain and Betivere in speed and spectacle. Over one hundred blows were exchanged by the two Lords and friends. Belvidere did not have the stamina he once knew and fell over after an ill-advised lunge.

And so Uriants was the last. Many, indeed most of nobles and commoners of the Land believed that Uriants would someday, eventually be King.

He was the richest and most powerful of all the Lords and had the most property. His vast wealth allowed him to maintain a standing army which gave him even more power and his skill and cunning in battle was legendary.

He was ten years younger than Leon des Gras and never felt stronger than he did at that precise moment. Perhaps he may not ascend the hill today for the chance at the Sword. But defeating Leon des Gras would assure him a second or perhaps even a third chance.

Even if Leon did manage to defeat him, he doubted his rival and friend would have the strength remaining to draw the Sword. As such, he would not have another chance to become King until the following year.

Even in the event of his defeat, all signs pointed to Uriants as the next King.

This duel would be longer and more fiercely fought of all the contests on that day; even the duel between Gawain and Betivere which was quickly becoming legend as the story of it was already being retold.

While the two great warriors slashed and parried each other, the shadow of the mountains and hills fell completely over the stadium.

For almost an hour, neither opponent could best the other either with brute strength or finesse. But when an opening did suddenly present itself, it was Leon des Gras it favored. He caught a wild strike from Uriants and was able to spin inside of it.

His body slammed into Uriants who started to fall but was so stubborn not to be defeated, he released his grasp of his sword and thrust his arms out to break his fall. Then in a move that even impressed Leon, Uriants regained his footing, took up a fighting stance and looked as if ready to box Leon des Gras for the victory or die in the attempt. He simply would not allow himself to lose.

He threw a few punches and kicked Leon on his shins and thighs. Leon, holding his own and Uriants' sword gave Uriants a quizzical look and said to him, "You can **not** be serious."

Suddenly realizing the foolishness of his position and behavior, Uriants finally allowed himself to acknowledge that he had lost. He stepped back from Leon and after a moment started to laugh.

"Alright," he said stretching out his arms as if inviting an embrace. "I'm willing to discuss terms of your surrender."

Leon des Gras joined his old friend in a laugh and an embrace while the spectators roared in approval. Looking at each other as if they'd shared the funniest joke they'd ever heard, the magnitude of the moment came to them both. Leon des Gras had defeated three opponents in a row. Now was his chance to become King.

Leon des Gras

At last his moment had finally come. Climbing the hill that had long ago been cleared of trees in order to provide a full view of the Sword from the tournament site, felt like a religious pilgrimage.

He thought he could feel the moment calling to him; the Sword itself beckoning him on. He knew that thousands were watching him from below but no one was allowed to follow; not even the Lords or even his own sons and daughter.

The sun had fallen behind the mountains but there was still enough light to see. Whether it was merely the moment or true, Leon des Gras would never be able to say for certain; but it appeared to him that the blade of the Sword shined as if the dawn were reflecting off of its steel.

His breathing became heavy and tears welled up in his eyes. With every step, the possibility of being King, something he'd dreamt of since before the Battle of Surranam felt as if becoming more and more within his grasp.

So many times, he'd felt that the crown was almost in his hands only to be defeated by another. Uther Pendragon had brought him down on the field of Surranam. Uriants and Belvidere had conquered him tournament after tournament; but now he had finally achieved what he believed destiny had been waiting to give him.

His heart pounded in his chest and there was a ringing in his ears. Every eye in the tournament site was fixed on this lone man inching closer and closer to the Sword and (they hoped) the throne. Even Arthur looked on with hope.

The Land was in need of a King and if his friends could not wear the crown, then this good and honorable man was more than worthy of it.

When he finally stepped up to the stone, all sensation except his sight had left him. He no longer felt the ground under his feet or the cool of the evening air. There was no sound; even the ringing in his ears and his own heart had gone silent.

As he prepared himself, he could see the shadow of Merlin looking on from the edge of the tree line. He stood in awe of both the moment and the beauty of the sight before him.

A golden hilt was affixed to the gleaming, silver blade and an almost common looking pummel sat atop the grip. In its simplicity it was more beautiful than any other weapon in the world.

When he finally felt like he was completely ready, he knelt before the stone, bowed his head and said a silent prayer; offering God his eternal loyalty and fidelity in exchange for the power to draw the Sword.

He then positioned himself in a manner he felt would best enhance his ability to lift a heavy object. His knees were bent and his back perfectly straight. He took the grip in both of his hands and he thought he felt a surge of power and strength. It served to reinforce his belief that God and destiny had chosen him for this moment.

He gambled that one, mighty motion would be what was required to pull the Sword. He pushed his legs hard into the ground and pulled with all his might, but the Sword did not budge. Seeing that he was not strong enough at first, he relaxed for a moment, repositioned his feet and tried again. Still, the Sword did not move.

Gasping for air from the strain of trying to lift the Sword and in desperation, he held the grip tighter; and at the same time he was trying to lift, he also tried shaking the Sword.

It would not move. He took a long, deep breath and gave it one more try. His legs burned, his shoulders started to hurt and he felt his back starting to give in. Finally, he lost his grip on the Sword and fell backward. In one single, awful moment, he realized the crushing truth that he had failed.

The crowds under the hill watched the drama unfold with excitement; only to be followed by disappointment. As Leon des Gras fell, they all felt that all of their hopes and dreams had been denied. Once more, there would be no King.

Arthur also felt a heavy disappointment; not only for the denial of a King, but he also hurt for this good and honorable man whom he felt that the spirits of the woods and the waters; even The One God himself had forsaken him.

The feeling of loss washed through the crowd like a wave, but was soon washed away by another. This was only the first day. Tomorrow someone else would have a chance. Perhaps then either the ancient spirits or the One God would hear their cry. A King would come.

Later

Guinevere was genuinely concerned about her father. Since being defeated by Excalibur as so many others had, he returned to his tent, posted two of his sons to stand guard and hadn't said a word to anyone.

Despite all her attempts to get through to Leon des Gras, he simply would not be accessible. She had never seen him like this before and she was deeply worried.

Despite her concern, she also recognized an opportunity when she saw one. Who better to get through to her father than his friend Bors the Elder of Callifax?

The two had been close for as long as she could remember and had seen each other through many awful events in their lives. He would be the perfect man for getting through to her father. And it didn't hurt that going to Bors might mean she could steal a few more minutes with Arthur.

As Guinevere arrived at Bors' campsite escorted by only six of her brothers, she simply could not restrain a broad smile upon seeing Arthur and even with a black eye, Arthur saw her as still the most beautiful girl he'd ever seen.

When Guinevere and her escort entered the campsite, Arthur stepped forward to greet her; however, he soon felt his father's iron hand clamp down on his shoulder. When he pulled Arthur back, the young man could clearly see the word "No" carved in every line on his father's face.

"He's not handling it well, is he?" Bors asked Guinevere.

"How did you know?"

"I remember the first time I tried to draw the Sword and it didn't budge. If he's feeling half the devastation I felt, he probably needs a hug."

As Bors started to leave with Guinevere and her entourage, Arthur called after him, "Perhaps I should go with you so you won't have to come back in the dark!"

"Nice try!" the Count replied.

The group of them which resembled a prisoner being escorted by soldiers was led by Bern, Leon's oldest son. Though not yet thirty, he had experienced more combat than Knights twice his age. These included campaigns against the Pith and the strange marauders who came from the sea every year.

It was an eerily quiet procession that made Guinevere uncomfortable even being escorted by six of her brothers and one of the most experienced Knights in all the Land. It was almost like the funerals she'd experienced in the years before or the dread she always felt when her father would annually visit the Lady Igrain of Cornwall.

When Bors the Elder stepped up to Leon's tent, the two guards crossed their pikes as a message to keep out. Bors looked at both young men (obviously the youngest in Leon's brood) with dark, intense eyes.

"One," He said in a warning voice. "Two..."

The two young men swallowed hard with fear and started to feel themselves shake. Whatever number series he was counting to did not seem to have a promising end for them.

"Two and a half..."

The two boys then felt a surge of relief when they heard their father announce, "Let him be."

Bors had seen the troubled expression on his friend's face so many times; he'd long lost count of the number. Leon des Gras was sitting with his side to the opening, his eyes fixed on a point that Bors could only imagine and his mouth covered by his hand.

"Did she have an escort this time?" Leon asked.

Bors already knew that Leon was referring to his daughter.

"She came with six of your sons; but I doubt it was her choice. She didn't seem too pleased about it."

"Was Bern with her?"

"He was."

"Good," Leon said somberly. "He'll make a fine Earl when the time comes."

"And when is that supposed to happen?" Bors said in a stern, but still gentle voice. "Is there something you haven't told me?"

"Nothing like that," Leon assured him. "Tonight, I feel I'm getting old I guess."

"I seem to remember warning you that the disappointment of failing to draw the Sword could be crushing."

Suddenly Leon became more animated.

"For God's sake, why do we have to go through this every year? Pulling an oversized toothpick out of a stone is no basis for a system of government."

"There's a little bit more to it than that."

"Don't be absurd. Even if someone does draw the Sword, Uriants would probably just kill him."

"You can't really believe that."

"It's a possibility."

Bors thought of dozens of things to say to argue with Leon, but stopped himself. He was there as a friend, not someone there for an argument.

He also knew that deep in his own heart, he suspected the same thing. He'd always known Uriants to be a good and fair man; a loyal friend. But he hungered for the crown above all other things. No one knew how far he would go to possess it.

"You'll have another chance," he said, still trying to console his friend.

"Not this year I won't," Leon reminded him.

The tradition was that once one had failed to draw the Sword, he could not even compete for the right to attempt it until the following year.

"And probably not the next either," he concluded.

"And what makes you say that?" Bors asked.

Leon answered with a heavy sigh that told Bors that his friend was started to come out of his disappointment and would be fine.

"I'm getting too old for this kind of thing," Leon said with resignation. "It's time for a new generation to start taking their place in this world. A younger King like Bern or your eldest might be better Kings as they're less likely to die in less than a year."

Thinking of Bors the Younger being King caused the older man to let a snort of laughter escape from him.

"I'm not sure my son is quite ready to be King," he told Leon.

The two shared a laugh and then spent the next hour or so sharing a flagon of beer from Leon's personal supply he'd brought with him.

They spoke of old times, battles won and women lost. They remembered old friends who were still with them and those who had passed.

After swallowing the last drop of beer in his flagon, Bors knew it was time to go. Just before stepping out of the tent, Leon said something very curious to him.

"I think that boy Arthur of yours might make a good King," Leon said seeming to pull the subject out of nowhere.

"He might," Bors acknowledged, "If only it was possible."

As previously arranged, Lord Uriants arrived at the ancient temple at precisely the moment the moon's light was directly above. He was alone, but unafraid of anything in the night. It was what waited him inside the temple that worried him.

Carefully walking over fallen stones and broken stairs, he made his way into the dark sanctuary. The only light came from a silvery beam of moonlight from the ceiling and precisely on the central altar.

Beside the altar was a man in shimmering chain mail and a white tunic that appeared to have never seen as much as a speck of dirt. Uriants knew better than this though.

The man wearing the tunic had performed many distasteful tasks for him. And tonight Uriants was going to ask him to perform the worst task he'd ever asked anyone to do on his behalf.

The man in the white tunic was kneeling before the altar as if in prayer. As Uriants cautiously approached, the other man slowly raised his head. Although he did not look at Uriants when he spoke, the Duke understood that he could be the only one he was talking to.

"Are you sure you want to do this?" The man asked. His voice echoed off of the large temple's walls almost as if in heavenly chorus.

"It has to be done," Uriants answered. "I've protected him from justice for far too long."

"Are you sure there's no other way?"

"If you don't want to do this, why don't you just say so?" Uriants growled.

"I neither want nor don't want to perform this task, but as always, I am always willing to execute true justice when others are unwilling."

"Then why ask...?"

"Before I perform this task," he continued, his eyes now looking straight into Uriants' soul, "I need to know that are prepared for the consequences to come."

Uriants thought for a moment and then nodded.

"Yes," he said as resolutely as he could. "I'm prepared."

"Then there's nothing left to discuss is there."

"Will you at least let me pay you something...?"

"I do not perform for money," the man said in an arrogant voice. "My skills will never be available to the highest bidder. What you want and what is too distasteful for you to do yourself is something that should have been done years ago; for had it been, no more innocents would have ever been harmed."

"I'm well aware of that," Uriants began to growl again.

"Then leave me to my task," the man finally said, "And know that yours is the only heart filled with guilt for it."

And so it was arranged Uriants thought to himself. He controlled his fear of what needed to be done and set the wheels in motion for it to happen.

He controlled his own guilt over the fate of his own brother. What he found difficulty with now were the feelings that none of this would have ever happened had not that stupid girl tempted her brother, even if unintentionally.

Even if she had been raped, he thought to himself, it would have been over quickly and she would not be mortally harmed. It was half her fault anyway. She needed to be taught a harsh, but necessary lesson. The worst feeling though, was the anger at that insolent boy putting his filthy hands on someone far above his station. How dare he?

The time would come, Uriants reasoned that he would have his revenge. Satisfying the need for vengeance was needed for true justice to be done. The guilty must be punished and that boy would pay dearly for causing all of this to happen.

"What Would Happen...?"

There were many traditions involved in the Midsummer Tournament. Arthur's favorite was the raising of the barn on the morning of the second day.

The young men who were either not qualified or still too young to be Knights would get together to raise a barn and construct throughout the day for the traditional barn dance set for the second night.

Arthur enjoyed this for several reasons; not the least of which was his affection for carpentry. Of all the chores he had to do around his father's castle and farm, carpentry was his favorite as it involved his meticulous nature, using large tools, hitting things and sawing things into smaller things.

There was also something internally satisfying about hard work that he enjoyed; especially when the finished product was well done. Many other youths didn't understand the attention to detail he put into the work; especially as another tradition was burning the barn to the ground on Midsummer Eve.

Bors the Elder had taught him that if he wasn't going to put all of his pride and skill into everything he did, he may as not do it all.

Every year since he was old enough to swing a hammer, he got to the project as soon as possible. One reason being that he was always excited by the project; another being that the earlier one got to working on the project, the earlier one could leave and have the rest of the day to one's self.

All young men between the ages of twelve and twenty one were required to work on the project for at least four hours or until the Master Builder told them they could go.

(Whining about wanting to leave usually ensured being bound to the project at least another two or three hours)

Arthur arrived just as the sky was starting to change colors and had even arrived before the lumber arrived.

No one, of course arrived before the Master Builder. Upon seeing Arthur, he smiled knowing that there would be at least part of the project done right.

He knew Arthur wasn't old enough yet, but in one more year, he would ask Bors the Elder to take the boy on as his apprentice. The boy was half-way to being a professional anyway and would earn a fine living as a Master.

With Bors the Younger already being the heir to the County, surely Bors the Younger would want his younger son to have the opportunity of a fine living earned on his own.

Arthur was put in charge of the front frame of the barn. This was a test from the Master Builder as this was one of the most important jobs of the project and to add difficulty, he put inexperienced boys to work with Arthur.

Not to the Master's surprise, Arthur was up to the challenge. When he inspected Arthur's work before the frame was to be raised, it was nearly perfect.

As the sun began to climb into the clear sky, the frames of the barn were pulled to the ground and then professional carpenters were lifted on harnesses to nail the frame together.

After this, a hearty breakfast was served to all those who showed up early enough to raise the frame. This would be the only free meal of the day and was another reason to show up as early as possible.

Arthur's least favorite tradition was the one he never seemed to avoid since he was nine. All of the Knights who had been eliminated on the first day patrolled the camp with their helmets in their hands asking for donations for the widows and orphans of fallen Knights (and to partially subsidize the beer available during the Barn Dance.)

The thousands of people who came to the tournament every year were known to be very generous and the helmets filled up rather quickly; especially just before the day's competition began.

To make room for more money and to relieve themselves of the responsibility of the money being in their possession, they would then deposit the coins in a large, burlap bag. As Arthur was known to be an honest and trustworthy lad (with nothing else to do as he had been early enough to the Barn Raising to have the rest of the day to himself), he would be selected and forced to mind the bag until the funds were collected and counted at the end of the day.

Despite what he thought to be his most clever plan of escape, Arthur had always been caught and given the bag. This year was no exception.

And so, he was seated in the tavern tent with the bag in his lap. Throughout the day, Knights came in, deposited their donations and received their (mostly) free beer in reward. The tavern master was the one who would be the first to count the money and he always subtracted the amount he felt he was owed for the beer.

The next to count was Artigan the Noseless who further subtracted the money that would be needed to pay the beer and ale venders and the last was Lord Uriants who knew that money had already been subtracted but had yet been able to actually catch anyone in the act of doing it.

Curiously, he'd had Arthur watched so carefully and so closely for so long, he found it ironic that the most likely person to steal the money (in his mind) was the most trustworthy.

This year, Uriants was so mad at Arthur, he had four armed guards surrounding the boy with orders to kill him immediately if Arthur so much put his hand in the bag. To Arthur's disappointment, none of the four were much conversation.

This still didn't stop one of the more clever attempts at stealing the bag that Arthur had yet seen. What had proven almost successful in previous years was to distract the throngs of people in one way or another and then to grab the bag from the poor, helpless boy left all alone in the tavern tent. Although severely frowned upon, attempting to steal the bag full of money had also become a "Tradition" at the Tournament.

These attempts included setting fire to a tent (which only worked twice), stampeding horses through the middle of the town, kicking a pregnant woman in the stomach to cause her to go into labor and stealing a sword belonging to a Knight which always caused every Knight not in the stadium to completely forget about the poor, helpless boy left all alone in the tavern tent.

What none of the thieves could ever seem to remember was that "The poor, helpless boy left alone in the tavern tent" was much cleverer than any of the other young men roped into the boring task.

He'd also proven smarter than the thieves.

Every time the diversion tactic was employed, Arthur would move the money bag to under his feet and replace the bag in his lap with a similar looking bag filled with something else; such as manure, slugs; and broken glass among other unsavory things to discover when simply reaching into the bag without looking (as they always did). Last year, he'd used three live snakes; but not poisonous as he didn't really want to hurt anyone. This year, he'd bought a dozen live crabs.

This year's diversion was a live, naked woman rushing through the middle of the town screaming and being chased by two men. It proved successful and every Knight and soldier went chasing after the three of them and everyone else just went to see what was going on.

What typically happened after that was that someone would run in, punch him in the face and be so much in a hurry that he would only grab the bag in his lap and not the bag under his feet. It usually left Arthur with a headache, but fortunately his nose hadn't been broken yet.

Today was different. The man punched him in the eye and then grabbed both bags.

"Damn!" Arthur blurted.

Realizing he'd been outsmarted, he had only one recourse. He'd have to chase the thief.

With everyone having chased the naked woman and her pursuers or crammed into the stadium, the path leading the opposite direction and eventually out of the campground was clear all the way to the barren hill.

Arthur ran after the thief, but not too fast. The thief was older and not in the best of athletic condition. Arthur could already see him begin to tire and knew that it was only a matter of time before the thief was his.

He anticipated at least one person popping out to attack him and was prepared when an assailant did appear. He put down the attacker with one good punch in the gut and a knee to the head. When he heard the footsteps of a second assailant though, he turned around and saw two more descending upon him.

Before these two could get to Arthur, one was tackled by Gawain who subdued his opponent with a head-butt that left his foe unconscious. Bors the Elder was less kind and he sliced off the third attacker's leg with one, clean swing of his blade.

Arthur hurriedly told them both," Thanks" and then returned to his pursuit.

He found the thief struggling up the hillside. Closing fast behind the prey, Arthur could already hear the man's labored breathing and it appeared as if the villain would fall at any second.

They passed the stone with the Sword and the thief could clearly go no further. He turned around and with a desperate look in his eyes, pulled a knife from out of his belt. Arthur simply smiled at him and said, "You're going to look awfully funny with that knife sticking out of your ass."

With Gawain and Bors the Elder having also climbed the hill and having drawn their weapons, the thief dropped both the bags and stumbled off into the forest.

Arthur, his father and Gawain all realized that there were likely more villains waiting in the forest in the hills and decided not to pursue.

There were two criminals already immobilized and Bors the Elder reasoned that after being questioned by Lord Uriants, they would lead Uriants' soldiers to any others who were part of the conspiracy to rob the money.

As Arthur and the other two gasped for breath, they started to laugh.

"I think they're getting cleverer every year," Arthur said in between shallow breaths.

As Gawain went to collect the bags, Bors the Elder teased both the young men, asking them, "What are you two huffing and puffing about? When I was your age, I could have ran up this hill with both of you tied to my back and still overtaken the rogue."

"In three feet of snow, no doubt," Arthur added.

Suddenly Gawain shouted, "What the devil?"

Arthur looked to him and saw him draw his hand out of one of the bags with a large crap clamped on to his hand.

"I suppose I should have warned you about that," Arthur told him.

The three men caught their breath and joked a little while longer, until Bors the Elder, with the money bag in his hand started down the hill.

"Oy!" Arthur called after Gawain who had left the other bag on the ground. "I paid good money for those crabs."

"You mean I paid good money for them," Bors responded. "Pick them up if you please. I don't like my money being wasted.

Gawain started following Bors, but Arthur had a funny feeling for a moment. He felt something wash over him like a wave but didn't quite whether it was an emotion or a sensation he'd never known before.

He also thought he saw Merlin out of the corner of his eye, but when he looked directly at where he thought Merlin was, the Wizard was gone. Arthur then dismissed the funny feeling and shook his head to get the image of Merlin out of his head.

He started to follow Bors and Gawain, but found himself stopping just in front of the Sword. A slightly mischievous thought then occurred to him. "What would happen if I tried to draw the Sword?"

It was an entertaining thought at the moment. He'd never given a moment's thought to the possibility of drawing the Sword and had never in his wildest dreams thought of being King. Yet, here he was; not more than two feet from the coveted Excalibur. Why waste the chance to have a moment of fun?

He took one step toward the Sword and almost stopped himself. He wasn't a Knight and hadn't won the right to attempt the Sword through combat. It didn't seem right.

But what would be the harm, he wondered? It wasn't likely that he'd actually pull the Sword out of the rock. No one else had; not even the strongest Knights and Lords in the land. "But what would happen…" He wondered.

He scoffed for a moment, then looked both ways to see if anyone was watching. Bors and Gawain were already half-way down the hill and not paying him any attention. And it never occurred to him that anyone in the stadium was either watching or cared.

"Oh, why not?" He asked himself.

He decided just to give it a little tug; just to see what would happen. He wrapped both of his hands over the grip, looked again to see that no one was watching. He then gave one little pull. To his surprise, the blade came flying out of the stone.

It came out so quickly and easily, he nearly dropped it. As the Sword came free, it made a loud ringing sound, like a high-pitched bell and the blade was so silvery bright, it almost seemed as if it was glowing.

A thousand thoughts suddenly raced through his mind and none of them good. He felt like he did when he was a little boy and had broken something and knew that if he didn't cover up the accident, he would get in serious trouble.

Hundreds of things to do came to mind and one solution seemed wiser than any other and that was to put the Sword back in the stone before he was caught. When he heard someone from the stadium cry out, "LOOK!!" he knew he was too late. He was busted.

No Way Out

For the first time in his entire life, Arthur saw his father speechless. Bors the Elder was looking at him with a shocked expression. His mouth was wide open but no words were coming out.

This was not a good sign.

Gawain too look amazed and horrified at the same time. For sixteen years, the strongest and bravest Knights and Lords in the Land had fought for the right to draw Excalibur from the stone and even the mightiest had failed.

But now Arthur, the seventeen year old squire of Bors the Elder, someone who could never even hope to touch the Sword was holding it in his hands. All three simply stood staring at each other until Arthur finally said, "I really wish someone would say something right now."

"What have you done?" Gawain helplessly answered.

Just then, Arthur noticed what looked like the entire campground moving toward and up the barren hill.

"Gentlemen," Arthur said trying to remain calm, "I could really use some advice right now."

Bors the Elder was still stunned and unable to speak. Arthur could never know the impact of what he'd just done, he thought. He felt as if several worlds were now crashing down upon him.

Gawain wondered what any of this could possibly mean. Was Arthur, a young man he'd known since childhood and who seemingly had no ambition of his own now King? He wasn't even a Knight. He was essentially a servant. How could he possibly be King?

As the people from the campground started inching their way up the steep hill, a horse came thundering to the top. To Arthur's dismay, it was Leon des Gras, the man who had failed to draw the Sword just one day earlier.

He too had the same expression of a fish having just been pulled from the water. As he climbed off his black horse and slowly started to approach Arthur felt the first signs of panic starting to creep up on him.

"Gentlemen," Arthur pleaded again, "I'm not kidding. I could really use some advice."

But then Leon des Gras did something that, on the surface seemed to be a good sign, but also indicated something even more horrifying. The powerful Earl of Blackpool dropped to one knee.

Several other Knights began to follow suit as did most of the spectators. It then became even more obvious to Arthur that he had gotten into deep trouble.

"I'm not sure I'm comfortable with you doing that," Arthur told Leon des Gras. His confidence of the reality of the situation didn't improve when he saw his own father doing the same thing.

"This is starting to get a little creepy."

At that moment, another horse ran up to the top of the hill and it carried someone who, finally Arthur thought had a reaction he could understand. Lord Uriants reached the top of the barren hill, his eyes burning with anger.

The Duke of Westphalia trembled with rage. The Sword had clearly been drawn by someone who did not have the right to even try.

Despite being of noble blood, the boy was only a squire. The best he could hope for in his lifetime would be to manage the Callifax family farm. To even touch Excalibur was far above his natural place in life.

But it wasn't just any lowly squire. It was "that boy" who seemed to be popping up all the time. First, he had instigated a brawl on the first night.

More insulting than that, he'd dared put his hands on a noble Knight. It didn't matter that the boy was defending a young lady. The boy had insulted Uriants' family and honor. Now he further insulted Uriants by claiming the prize he knew was rightfully his. He'd seen enough.

"You miserable worm!" He spat at Arthur in between clenched teeth. "What have you done?"

"I would think that's fairly obvious," he said, trying to defuse the situation.

"Do you really think this is funny?" The Duke growled. "How dare you?"

"I'd be more than willing to give you the Sword if you want it," Arthur heard himself say; and quickly realized that it may have been the dumbest thing he'd ever said.

"Are you now trying to make me part of your sick prank?" Uriants shouted. "By God, I've had enough of this," he grunted as he drew his sword. "I'm going to end this here and now!"

Uriants started to march toward Arthur and raise his sword to attack. At that point, Leon des Gras intervened. He jumped in front of Uriants and pushed him back.

"Put your sword away this instant!" Leon barked at Uriants. "Can you not see?" And then in a near worshipful voice, he added, "He has drawn the Sword from the stone. He is King."

"That really doesn't help me," Arthur mumbled.

"Leon des Gras is right," Bors the Elder added, to the disappointment of Arthur.

His voice was strange. It seemed full of pride and awe, but there was also a hint of sadness and regret. Arthur looked to his father to see him still on one knee and tears starting to well up in his eyes.

"He is King."

"Have you both completely lost your senses?" Uriants asked angrily. "This boy can **not** be King! He's a squire! He has no right even touching the Sword.

"But he has," Leon added. "God has chosen him. He is King and we owe him our allegiance."

"I owe him nothing!" Uriants hissed.

Uriants raised his sword again and looked ready to charge. Leon des Gras then drew his own weapon and stood directly in front of Uriants to stop him.

"Get out of my way Leon," Uriants warned his friend. "You know I have to do this."

"No!" Bors shouted as he drew his sword. "I will not have you become an assassin."

"It's an execution not a murder!" Uriants spat again. "He has betrayed us all with some magic trick and now he means to bring us all to our knees. I will not bow to a squire!"

The crowd that had gathered around the site now started to join in the argument and take sides. Most were starting to shout and scream "He is King!" and "At last, God has given us a King!" Still others were calling Arthur "Thief!" and "imposter!" Some even shouted, "He is in league with the devil!"

"Don't make me your enemy," Uriants warned Leon des Gras. "You know I will not hesitate to do the worst I am capable of to preserve what is right."

"If raise you your sword one more time at the new King, you make an enemy," Bors said as he stood next to Leon.

Shouts and cries from the crowd started to turn into arguments. Soon people in the crowd started pushing and shoving. Uriants looked at his two oldest friends like a predator about to pounce. Leon des

Gras and Bors the Elder raised their own swords as they prepared to defend themselves.

Arthur then felt a firm and icy hand grab his arm and say, "Come with me."

Everything went dark for an instant; less than a blink of an eye. Arthur then found himself in a completely different place. He seemed, he thought to be in the hall of a castle.

Surprised and stunned he looked about the hall as if waiting for someone to attack him and held Excalibur prepared to defend himself. Then a smooth, rich voice which seemed to echo from every wall called to him, "Welcome home Arthur Pendragon."

Revelations

The voice Arthur heard came from behind him. He spun around, continuing to hold the Sword as if ready to defend himself. There he saw a stone staircase winding up along a wall. At the top of the stairs stood Merlin, whom Arthur easily recognized despite the Wizard's hood covering his head and half of his face.

"I should have known you'd be behind this," Arthur said angrily. "I hope you don't think this is funny."

"Oh no, My Gracious Lord," Merlin told Arthur as he seemed to float down the stairs. "This is no joke. I have brought you home so that I may prepare you for the difficult tasks ahead."

"This doesn't look like Pembrook Castle," Arthur said, now pointing the blade of Excalibur directly at Merlin.

"It isn't," the Wizard answered. "This is Dragonhearth in the Duchy of Drachenheim; the ancestral home of the House of Pendragon."

"That's lovely, but it doesn't explain why I'm here or why in the devil you just called me 'Arthur Pendragon.'"

"I have explained why I brought you and I called you by the name of the House of Pendragon because that's who you are; who you really are."

"I don't particularly like riddles," Arthur said raising the sword slightly. The Wizard was still coming towards him. "Especially the ones I can't solve."

As the Wizard stepped closer, he pulled back the hood of his cloak and revealed a face that somehow appeared to be gentle and sinister at the same time. His green eyes were so bright, it almost looked like they were glowing and his snow white hair was pulled back into a long pony tail.

"This is no riddle, My Lord," Merlin said.

"I really wish you wouldn't call me that."

"But that is the proper way to address you now."

"There are a hundred reasons I can list off the top of my head why that's ridiculous."

A sly smile creeped across Merlin's face.

"You are the son of Uther Pendragon and the Lady Igrain, Duchess of Cornwall and it is now time for you to claim your birthright as Duke of Drachenheim and the rightful heir to the throne."

Arthur was a little taken aback by this statement and unsure of what to say until he finally told Merlin emphatically, "Bullshit!"

Merlin smiled as if he was the sole guardian of a secret and started to circle somewhat melodramatically around Arthur.

"How many of the strongest and most powerful Knights and Lords of the Land have tried to draw the Sword that now rests in your hands?" He asked the young man.

"I haven't exactly been keeping score," trying once more to defuse another difficult situation.

"In the last sixteen years since the Midsummer Tournament began, exactly thirty four men have tried to lift the Sword and not even Galbreath the Giant, who won the right to attempt it last year wasn't strong enough. Almost every Knight and Lord in the Land has tried to draw Excalibur at least once and none have succeeded. So how do you think it's possible that a lowly squire was able to accomplish what the mightiest could not?"

Arthur's attention and focus was distracted by the question; but Arthur knew that the Wizard who was notorious for only telling people half the truth could be trying to trick him for some reason.

"I have been watching you for many years," Merlin added. "You've grown strong and brave like your father, Uther. You even look like your father except for the blonde hair. And what has been growing in your mind up to this point has been the beginning of Wisdom. You will make a fine King, even better than your father."

"My father," Arthur said defiantly, "Is Bors the Elder Count of Callifax."

"Uther's dying words before setting the Sword into the stone were 'No one but my own blood shall have Excalibur' and the Sword always obeys its master."

"That cannot be true," Arthur insisted. "I have never known any father but mine."

"That's because I took you from your mother's arms when you were an infant."

There was something in those words that struck Arthur deep. They stirred a deep and hidden memory that was little more than a brief image. He'd seen it in dreams or in a picture that flashed only for an instant when he closed his eyes; sometimes only when he blinked. He'd never been able to see it clearly before.

However, now the image came closer in to focus. He remembered the face of a beautiful woman with shining blonde hair.

"Why would you do that?" Arthur heard himself ask in a whisper.

"Plots had already been put in motion to assassinate your father," Merlin answered somberly. "Had I left you with your mother or Uther, you would have been killed as well."

More images started to come into focus for Arthur. He remembered an image and a feeling of him being torn away from something. He could hear crying and wailing.

"Though I must confess that this happened a little sooner than I expected," Merlin continued. "But now that what was meant to happen has happened, there's no turning back. You are the son of the King and his rightful heir. It is time for you to take your place in history."

The Empty Castle

Merlin disappeared as suddenly as he'd appeared. This served to prove that it was indeed the enigmatic Magician as he had the reputation for doing so.

This left Arthur alone, or so he thought in an immense stone castle that he had just been told was his "Ancestral home." But it couldn't possibly be true, Arthur reasoned. His father was Bors the Elder of Callifax and as far as Arthur knew, his father was incapable of even contemplating being dishonest.

Besides, Arthur continued to ponder; how could I be in one part of the Land one second and then seemingly on the opposite side of the world the next? He knew Merlin was rumored to be a powerful Wizard; but surely there are laws of nature that even he must obey.

Still, Arthur thought, there was a ring of truth in what Merlin had told him. For one thing, Merlin also had the reputation for honesty when asked direct questions; "A bit too honest," he'd heard his father say. Merlin did, however have a reputation for only telling people what he wanted to know and not always the full truth.

As Arthur finally started getting over the twin shocks of suddenly appearing in a castle he didn't recognize and being told that his parents were two people he'd never met, he started to feel curious about this castle that supposedly belonged to him. Many questions were still going through his mind and the person to answer them was nowhere to be seen.

Arthur felt confident that the room he was in at the moment was likely a hall of some sort; perhaps even the "Great Hall" of a high-ranking Lord. It was certainly big enough. The space between the four walls appeared to be enough to swallow smaller castles, like Pembrook whole.

There were overturned chairs and tables and one single long table at the far end of the hall. This table was broken and splintered in what looked like the results of a long ago battle. The walls were decorated with deer antlers, boar's heads and various weaponry and armor.

At the same far end as the shattered table was a large standard above where Arthur presumed the Lord of the Manor would sit at his table. Most of it was covered in cob webs and years of dirt. Arthur felt strangely drawn to it and stepping through the debris all around him, he soon was directly underneath it.

He carefully brushed aside the dust and dirt and the standard fully revealed itself. It was black with the images of five dragons facing each other in a circle. It didn't necessarily prove what Merlin had told him to be fact; but this was indeed the flag of the House of Pendragon.

Still surveying the damage in the hall, Arthur noticed a small doorway in the corner of the side of the hall near the wrecked table. It was dark beyond the door, but there were lit torches that Arthur thought Merlin must have left. He took one of the torches and decided to explore beyond the doorway.

At the doorway, he found the remnants of a thick wooden door that had obviously been broken down as it was little more than splinters. Beyond that was winding stairwell with stone steps. He followed it down still wondering what had happened in this place.

Littering the stairs were the remains of people whose only remnants were their bones. Arthur found himself disturbed by the fact that none of them were wearing armor or had weapons near them. These were innocents, he thought to himself. Why were they slaughtered?

At the bottom of the stairs, he found what appeared to be a large kitchen. Most of the long tables were overturned and a few rats scurried away as he entered. Dug into one wall was a large, open fire pit not unlike a fireplace. There were several spits scattered around the floor and another was found near another skeleton in civilian clothing who had perhaps tried to use the spit as a weapon. Whatever battle the dead man fought he'd clearly lost.

Using the torch to continue to look around the kitchen, he found one table standing up with several wicker baskets and bottles standing on it. Upon closer inspection, he found the baskets filled with bread, fresh meat and eggs and opening one of the bottles, he found it filled with wine.

"Looks like someone's been shopping," Arthur said aloud, assuming he was alone.

A woman's voice echoed off of the stone walls telling him, "He told us you were coming."

Still nervous and wary, Arthur spun around quickly holding both the torch and the Sword in the direction of the voice.

Three people stood in the kitchen just inside the door; an older man, woman and a young woman appearing to be in her twenties. They were clearly no threat as they only stood staring at him; but though a little more relaxed, Arthur still wasn't completely comfortable at seeing them.

"I really wish you wouldn't sneak up on me like that," he told the three of them.

"Begging your pardon. My Lord," the woman said to Arthur as she cautiously stepped up to him. "But the Wizard asked us to come so that we could serve you in whatever capacity we may."

Setting the torch in a holder, he told the woman, "I'm nobody's Lord."

"Oh but you are, My Lord," she insisted. "You're the spitting image of your father, The Duke; except for the blonde hair that is."

Although not afraid, but still keeping his distance, Arthur told her, "I suppose you're going to tell me that I'm the son of Uther Pendragon and I'm the Duke of Drachenheim."

"You most certainly are, My Lord," She explained. "You even have the birthmark."

"What birthmark?"

The woman smiled and blushed a little.

"Given its location, I doubt you've ever seen it."

"And where would that be?"

The young woman giggled and blushed, making it clear to Arthur where the birthmark was likely located.

"I see," he said feeling a little embarrassed. "And how is it that you managed to see it?"

"Well," the woman told Arthur, "When the Wizard brought you here three days ago…"

"Three days?" Arthur interrupted. "I was at the Midsummer Tournament site an hour ago."

"I'm afraid that's a bit complicated, My Lord. I think it's best the Wizard explain it to you."

Arthur thought about questioning her more on this subject; but it was obvious she didn't have any answers.

"Anyway," She continued. "When the Wizard brought you here, your clothes were in an awful state and needed to be washed."

"And you didn't wash them with me in them, did you?"

"Not exactly," she said as gently as she could.

Arthur ended that conversation with a resigned, "Lovely."

The Ancestral Home

Arthur learned the names of the three people and that they were former servants of the House of Pendragon. The older woman and man were Elsbeth and Ascher respectively and the younger woman was Rachel. Elsbeth was Ascher's sister and Rachel had a different story than theirs.

Elsbeth took Arthur on a brief tour of the castle and Ascher told him so much about its history, he'd already forgotten most of it. The large hall in which he found himself was indeed the Great Hall. Ascher spoke of great feasts and ceremonies; but also funerals and courts where justice was not always dispensed equally.

Prior to Uther, the House of Pendragon had a reputation of favoritism and corruption; including unfair taxation where the Lords of Drachenheim divided people into tax "Classes." The merchant and tenant classes were taxed nearly twice as much as the wealthy landowners and the tenant farmers had to pay unfair taxes in addition to having half of their crops seized by the Duke and still more was seized by the local Counts who owned the land on which the farmers worked.

"Lord Uther changed all that," Ascher explained. "The previous Duke Dohn died when Uther was only sixteen and when Uther became master here, he changed everything.

"He changed many of the laws, including instituting standard punishments for criminals. In the old system, those who were found guilty of crimes could be punished according to the will of the local magistrate or Count and some of the things they came up with were quite ghastly.

"Your father established an appeals process where those in the duchy could bring complaints all the way to the Duke if need be. He also created a new tax in which all who earned money had to give the same percentage of their wealth. He'd even started to build housing for the sick and the lame so that they could be looked after. This was to be the law of the Land, but Lord Uther died before any of that could happen."

After the brief tour, the three of them found places to sit and rest in the library while they ate a meal prepared by Rachel. The library had also been torn apart with bookshelves having been emptied and books thrown to the floor like garbage. All of the couches and chairs in the library had been cut open and almost everything else had been utterly destroyed.

"What happened here?" Arthur asked during the meal.

"What do you mean, My Lord?" Elsbeth asked.

"It looks as if someone went out of their way to destroy almost everything inside these walls."

Arthur then noticed a terrified expression cross over Rachel's face, who then quickly almost ran out of the library.

"Was it something I said?" Arthur asked.

"Oh it's not your fault, My Lord," Elsbeth answered. "Terrible times followed Lord Uther's death."

"Knights commissioned by some of the other Lords and rogue Knights came pouring into Drachenheim after Lord Uther's death. They came to the castle looking for treasure and destroyed everything in their path. They broke into every room and chamber, took down tapestries and burned them; they even demolished several walls looking for the riches they thought were hidden somewhere in the castle."

"I read about the famous treasure of Dragonhearth and I can understand how the lust for gold can cause men to acts of evil. But why kill the servants?"

Elsbeth looked far away as if looking back on horrible moments and looking away from them at the same time.

"A funny thing happens when people get the taste of blood in their mouths," She said sadly. "One man or woman can be perfectly reasonable, but when you multiply the bloodlust of over a hundred men and women alike, devastation follows."

Arthur saw tears begin to well in Elsbeth's eyes.

"Rachel was one of the daughters of Lord Uther's cousins and only five years old at the time," she explained. "When the Knights came, they were only interested in the gold mostly. But the people from the towns and villages came for revenge on the House of Pendragon for the generations of injustice they had perpetrated. They killed everyone that breathed. Ascher and I found poor Rachel underneath a pile of corpses and covered in blood.

"I don't think we'll ever know what happened to her. She's never spoken a word since the day we found her."

"Every man and woman in the House of Pendragon were slaughtered like animals and it was thought the bloodline had ended. But blessed be, you came along. Now the duchy can be restored."

Later, Arthur was shown to a room in the castle that had been damaged the least. It was the only one that still had a mattress; although the bed's frame had been ruined.

"The three of you won't sleep on the floor tonight will you?" Arthur protested.

"Oh no My Lord," Elsbeth told him. "We live in a cottage on the estate and will be most comfortable."

"We were going to invite you to stay with us," Ascher added. "But we only have two beds. For you to stay with us would mean one of us having to sleep on the floor. We'll do it if you wish..."

"That's quite alright," Arthur cut him off. "I should be alright for one night."

After the three of them had left, Arthur found himself alone in the castle again. The mattress was on the floor and he thought that it too must have been cleaned in some way. It didn't smell like seventeen years of dirt and mildew.

He had trouble sleeping as so many thoughts and questions continued to race through his mind.

Foremost in his thoughts was imagining the awful scene that had to have happened when the castle was invaded and unspeakable acts committed. He tried not to think about what had happened to Rachel, but he couldn't keep it out of his mind.

There were other concerns as well. What had happened at the campsite? It looked as if a war was about to start and three men who had once been the best of friends looked ready to attack one another. What had happened? What was going to happen now that Excalibur had been drawn?

And how the blazes did he get to Dragonhearth castle?

The Next Day

As the sunlight came pouring in through the open windows of the room in which he slept, Arthur squirmed and tried to turn away from the light to capture just a few more moments of blessed sleep. Finding a comfortable position on the unusually soft mattress, he thought he felt another person's breath on his face. This was not usual.

His eyes blinked open and the face of the young woman Rachel came into focus. She was sleeping comfortably on the mattress next to him and the fact that she wasn't supposed to be there caused Arthur to nearly jump out of the bed. This woke up the young woman and she got to her feet as fast as possible.

Arthur saw the terror in her face and as she ran to the doorway, he called after her, "Wait, wait, wait!"

To his surprise, he'd also ran around the mattress almost as if trying to catch her and this apparently didn't make things better.

Looking as if in a state of panic, she backed herself into a corner and looked ready to run through Arthur if necessary to get away from him.

I'm not going to harm you!" Arthur shouted.

She looked at Arthur with wild eyes, almost like an animal and Arthur was suddenly reminded of the horrors she must have experienced as a child.

Arthur stood in front of her, but then took a step back to try and reassure her of his intentions. She did appear to relax a little and Arthur told her, "I promise, I'm not going to hurt you."

She appeared to relax a little more and Arthur told her softly, "I just wasn't expecting to wake up next to you. I'm sorry if I startled you."

Elsbeth then came running into the doorway, breathing heavily herself.

"What's going on?" Elsbeth asked in between gasps of breath. "What's happened?"

"Nothing's happened," Arthur said as calmly as he could. "I woke up next to an unexpected, but not unwelcome guest."

"Unexpected guest?" Elsbeth asked.

She looked to Rachel who was much calmer, but now looking embarrassed.

"How did she wind up in your bed?" Elsbeth asked in a slightly accusatory tone.

"I'm not sure," Arthur answered. "But you can rest assured that nothing dishonorable occurred."

Elsbeth, still looking like a mother protecting her children, asked Rachel, "Is this true?"

Rachel nodded her head and Elsbeth appeared more relaxed.

"Breakfast will be ready in a few moments," Elsbeth told the two of them.

Rachel shuffled out of the room, still looking embarrassed and Elsbeth soon followed.

Arthur was alone in the room and everything that had transpired recently, slowly started to return to his thoughts. It wasn't a dream.

He really was in a castle and not his little tent on the Surranam plane at the tournament site. The events that had seemed like a nightmare apparently did happen and the sword Excalibur was in his hand; though at the moment he wasn't really sure how.

Arthur came down the stairs and into the library wrapped in the blanket he had slept under the night before.

"Are you cold, My Lord?" Ascher asked him.

"Just a bit," Arthur answered.

The wreckage of the library was easier to see Arthur noticed. He could see more smashed tables, chairs and couches, the floor was littered with books and there were gashes in the bookshelves where someone apparently had tried to hack through them.

"I'll get a fire going in the Great Hall," Ascher told him and started to leave.

Arthur stopped him by saying it wasn't necessary.

"I've never known it to be so cold in summer," Arthur noted.

"Oh, it's not summer," Elsbeth told him. "It's October."

Arthur thought for a moment of asking how in the world it was suddenly October when the last he remembered was the day before Midsummer's Eve, but decided against it.

That conversation would likely only lead to more uncomfortable questions and answers which Arthur wasn't prepared for just yet; at least not before breakfast.

After a nice breakfast and some pleasant conversation, Arthur did finally say something that was starting to bother him.

"I'm surprised they didn't burn the castle down."

"This castle will never burn," Ascher said almost reverently.

"There were many warlike days long ago when the Pendragon family fought one another for control. One Duke would replace another slain and one cousin or brother would murder another. But this castle has stood for three hundred years. Before Uther's death, there were many attempts to burn it to the ground, but no fire would ever consume it."

Sometime later, Arthur felt like exploring again and toured the castle in parts he hadn't yet seen. Even in a state of destruction and with bones still strewn about the floors and walls, it was an impressive castle.

Arthur followed stairs up to four levels and found immense rooms along with servants' quarters that he thought fit for a Count. Through open windows, many of them with the shutters destroyed he saw thick walls surrounding the manor with battlements looking over rolling hills.

Through one window, he saw a large city off to the south and staring out to it, he heard footsteps coming in to the room he was in.

It was Ascher and his timing seemed perfect as Arthur had more questions to ask.

"Is that Camelot?" Arthur asked.

"It is indeed My Lord," Ascher told him. "It was once the jewel of Drachenheim with roads leading from it to all the cities and towns of the Land."

"That's convenient," Arthur joked.

"It was always meant for Camelot to be the capital city of this realm; but the Knights and Lords could never decide upon a King until Uther. Even when Uther did earn the throne, he didn't live long enough to unite the Land under his banner."

"Are there still people living there?" Arthur asked.

"There are," Ascher answered. "But it's not what it once was. Merchants and travelers no longer journey to this land from other counties and duchies, so there's very little trade.

"There are farms and fields, but the Counts all hoard everything in counties they rule over as if they were Kings of their own nations. Camelot is a den of thieves and cutthroats. The only people sleeping within the city are those on the run or hiding."

Arthur began to feel a little sad at this story for Camelot was once legendary for its wealth and power. The Lords of Drachenheim had allegedly earned a vast fortune and the whole world seemed to revolve around what had once been a center of commerce and culture.

As more questions started to fill his mind, Arthur noticed something out of the corner of his eye. There appeared to be a black mass moving from Camelot in the direction of the castle. Closer inspection revealed that the mass was made of hundreds of people walking to the castle.

"Does the castle have a gate?" Arthur asked.

"It used to," Ascher answered.

"Let me guess," Arthur said dryly. "It was smashed long ago."

"I'm afraid so, My Lord."

"Lovely."

Pilgrims and Politicians

The Sword was in Arthur's hand again. This he found particularly unsettling as this time he knew he'd set it down and intentionally not picked it up. In fact, it was his specific purpose to leave the Sword behind as he wasn't sure greeting hundreds of people at the gates of a castle and wielding a longsword would make a good impression.

He'd asked Ascher to show him the way to the main entrance inside the perimeter walls and felt fortunate that he did as he knew that he would have too easily become lost in the castle's labyrinth of corridors and tunnels. Once outside the main entrance though, he noticed that Ascher was no longer following him.

"Am I correct in assuming you're not going to greet our guests with me?" Arthur asked him.

"I think I'd prefer to stay here, My Lord," Ascher replied. "Ever since the last time Dragonhearth was visited by this many people, I'm rather uncomfortable in crowds."

Arthur couldn't argue with that.

Before he reached the main gate, Arthur saw that at least thirty men and women were already inside the gate. Getting closer to them, he noticed that most of them had a strange expression on their faces; somewhere in between religious worship and terror; neither one of which Arthur was fond of seeing at the moment.

Arthur was standing at the top of stone steps leading up to the manor. The men and women looking up at him were both pleasant and worrying as he couldn't remember anyone having been that apparently happy to see him before.

It was unsettling as there was something rather unnatural about the attention they were paying him; especially as the people weren't saying anything to or about him. They were just standing there looking up at him.

"Good morning!" Arthur called down to them in as pleasant a voice as he could manage.

There was no response or reaction from the people gawking at him.

"It's a bit chilly this morning."

Still nothing.

"Does anyone think it might rain?"

After a few more uncomfortably silent moments, one man stepped forward to the bottom of the steps wearing an even more reverent expression than any of the others. He stopped at the very bottom steps and with his eyes appearing to well up with tears slowly eased himself down to one knee.

"Hail Arthur!" He shouted. "Hail to our new King!"

These were not the words Arthur was hoping someone would say to him at this early hour in the day. He felt similarly disturbed when many in the crowd also shouted, "Hail! Hail! Hail!"

"That's very kind of you..." Arthur tried to say, but still more voices started shouting at him.

"How can we serve you My Lord?" One would ask.

"Command us in all things My Lord! We are your humble servants!"

Still another shouted, "Praise be to the King that God has finally given us!" This was followed by another chorus of "Hail! Hail! Hail!"

Though not comfortable with the situation he now faced, Arthur wasn't particularly afraid. They didn't seem likely to attack him; especially as most of them were kneeling.

But he still didn't think that this adulation was a good thing; especially as he fully understood that there may be those who weren't quite as glad to see him.

Most of the crowd was still shouting "Hail!" and Arthur wished they would stop. He raised his hand and implored the crowd to, at least stop shouting at him; but the noise had grown so loud that he couldn't hear his voice.

In an instant, he felt a strange vibration in his sword hand and this was followed by an ear-piercing ringing sound coming from the blade of Excalibur. Some of the crowd screamed and some started to run; but when the Sword stopped screaming, everyone quickly calmed down. To Arthur's relief, they had finally quieted down to where he could talk to them.

"Thank you!" He called down to the then larger crowd looking up at him. He also looked at the Sword as if to ask it how it managed to do that.

"So," He tried again. "Good morning. Thank you for coming."

"We have come to offer our loyalty and fidelity to our new King and Lord," The first man that spoke said to Arthur.

Arthur paused for a second before saying, "About that...I think we should have a little discussion..."

"Long have we prayed for this moment to come, Gracious Lord," a voice from the back of the crowd shouted up.

"Long have we longed for a King to rise and restore the oneness of the Land and her people," A woman in the front shouted.

"All hail Arthur; our new and forever King!"

The hails and chants started sounding again and Arthur felt like the Sword was about to do something again, but one voice rose above the crowd.

"No! No! No!" Cried out a loud and angry voice. "You fools! Have you all completely lost your minds?"

The voice belonged to a tall and robust man wearing finer linens than most of the people in the courtyard and Arthur reasoned that he must have been a merchant.

"This is no King!" he shouted. "He's a fraud! An imposter! He's come to make fools and slaves of us all!"

"I assure you sir that is not my intention…"Arthur tried to tell him, but the man would not listen.

"He's here to bring back the oppression of the House of Pendragon back on our backs!"

This man's voice was soon joined by others shouting, "He's right! He's no King!"

A voice in the back shouted, "He'll take our lands!" Another yelled, "He'll throw us from own homes!" And Arthur was not surprised at all when someone shouted, "He'll take our daughters and make whores out of them!"

To this, Arthur simply mumbled to himself, "I was wondering when someone would get around to saying that."

The merchant then turned back to Arthur and told him with clenched teeth, "Even if he is a King, we don't need him! We've done just fine without a King since the House of Pendragon was wiped out and I, for one will be a slave to no one!"

The crowd then erupted with the noise of those who welcomed Arthur and those who didn't started to turn on one another. The shouting turned angrier and angrier, leading inevitably to pushing and shoving. The Merchant then picked a large scythe and started to charge up the steps shouting, "By God, I'll make sure he's no King!"

Arthur prepared to defend himself, but before the Merchant could reach him, Arthur heard the screaming of a horse. A huge, black stallion then leapt in front of Arthur and knocked the Merchant down the steps.

Arthur then followed the sound of the thundering of hooves and saw two Knights on horseback charging from the right of the crowd.

The crowd panicked and ran through the gates as quickly as possible while the two Knights positioned themselves to make sure none came back toward Arthur.

The stallion continued to stand in front of Arthur almost as if guarding him. When he did move aside, Arthur saw two men wearing very familiar tunics and armor, but he was still cautious. When they both removed their helmets, Arthur breathed a sigh of relief as Bors the Elder and his son stood before him.

A Squire No More

Arthur stepped down from the stone steps to greet his unexpected, but most welcome guests.

"Well, you certainly arrived at the right time," He said to them.

"We actually arrived late last night," Bors the Elder told Arthur. "Your servants managed to find a couple of rooms free of corpses and we only woke up about half an hour ago."

"The old woman told us about the crowd coming and we thought you could use some help," Bors the Younger added.

"I wish someone had told me you arrived," Arthur said smiling. "I might not have been foolish enough to try and take on the entire crowd by myself."

"It looks like you had some support," Bors the Elder commented. "But none of them had scythes."

"I'm sure Arthur could have handled him with ease," Bors the Younger said in a curious tone. Arthur had never heard his brother speak either to him or about him so complimentary.

"At this point," Bors the Elder continued, "It's a good thing he didn't have to. Who knows what would have happened if there had been bloodshed."

Arthur then felt the black horse nudge him on the head. Arthur looked to the horse and felt a strange connection as he stared into the stallion's eyes. In a way, it felt as if he could hear the steed speaking to him in a language only he and Arthur understood.

"And who do we have here?" Arthur asked.

"I'm not sure," Bors the Elder answered. "He's been following us for a month."

The revelation that they had been traveling for at least one month sounded strange to Arthur, but no stranger than anything else he'd recently learned.

"You know of course," Arthur told both of them, "That I'm naturally going to have to ask how you knew to find you here."

"I honestly don't know," The Elder answered. "We just did."

"Sounds like Merlin's work to me," The Younger added. To this, Arthur simply chuckled and said, "Doesn't surprise me at all."

The more Arthur looked into the stallion's eyes and stroked his neck, the more he seemed to know more about him. He felt that he could see the journey the horse had taken in order to reach Dragonhearth and his desire to be with Arthur.

He showed Arthur images of the woods and fields he had crossed for many weeks to complete a journey that he simply had to make.

"Severus," Arthur heard himself say aloud.

Looking to the two Bors', Arthur then told them, "That's his name; Severus."

"That's more than we know about him," The Elder said.

"I guess you didn't know how to ask," Arthur joked and they all laughed.

Arthur then started to walk toward the stables he had been shown the day earlier saying, "I guess I need to see to the horses then."

In that precise moment, Arthur remembered everything Merlin and the servants had told him and the questions that had been rattling around in his head returned.

He then looked to the man who had been his father for seventeen years and saw Bors the Elder looking both sad and guilty. Even with a thousand questions wanting to be asked at the same time, the only one he managed was, "I'm not your squire anymore, am I?"

Bors the Elder didn't say anything. He merely looked to the ground and sadly shook his head.

Arthur felt heavier and darker. That simple answer that the only father he'd ever known didn't say but still made clear proved everything the Wizard had told him. The entirety of the life he once knew suddenly came in to question as did everything he thought he knew. He turned to walk away and Severus followed.

Bors the Elder saw his son start to call after Arthur, but he stopped him.

"Leave him be for now," The older Knight told his son. "At times like these, a man needs to be alone."

After attending to Severus and to his pleasant surprise, Arthur found some precut lumber and carpentry tools left by the servant's entrance. Although he was slightly curious to their origins, he was more concerned about how much he felt he needed to be busy in order to clear his head.

While hauling the lumber and the tools through the huge castle and back to the room he had slept in the night before, he noticed his servants carrying skeletons and corpses through the same corridors.

He thought to ask them about what they were doing, but his mind was already occupied with the task he had laid out for himself for however long it would take.

Carpentry requires a lot of focus and attention to detail. Wood had to be cut to exact measurements and then sanded down into smooth edges.

Even though bed frames were among the easiest things to build, they still had to be exact specifications. One mistake would mean having to completely start over. Unfortunately, the task didn't take long enough and Arthur was finished long before he felt he needed to work.

Feeling that he needed more time to not think about everything in his head, he started and completed two more frames for the rooms for the men he had previously known as his father and brother.

As he didn't hear anyone approach from behind, he nearly jumped out of his skin when he heard the voice of Merlin tell him, "It's a pity really."

He jumped up and spun around and once more found Excalibur in his hand.

"When you become King," Merlin told him, "The world is going to lose an excellent carpenter."

"Do you always sneak up on people like that?" Arthur said with an angry growl.

"Not exactly like that," Merlin said in a humorous voice. "I have at least a hundred different ways of sneaking up on people.

Arthur looked curiously at the Sword and almost asked Merlin how it seemed to keep magically appearing in his hand, but thought better of it. One question of such a nature might lead to more questions he didn't want to know about at that moment.

"I'm not in a humorous mood Wizard," he warned Merlin. "I suggest you play your little games with someone else."

"You'll be happy to know then that I'm not here to play games," the Wizard answered.

"Whatever it is you want, tell me quickly. I've got a lot of work left to do."

"I'm actually here to do you a favor," Merlin said.

"And what favor would that be?"

"Prevent you from making a fool of yourself and make an already awkward situation more uncomfortable for everyone."

Arthur picked up a long piece of wood and began measuring it for one side of Bors the Younger's bed frame as if to give the impression he wasn't interested in what Merlin had to say.

"Does this have anything to do with the lie I've been living my entire life?" He asked.

"Oh it was no lie," Merlin informed him.

"No lie?" Arthur said, barely containing his desire to shout. "I just found out that the two people whom I believed to be family aren't who they claimed. They've been raising a bastard for seventeen years."

"Nothing could be further from the truth," Merlin said calmly.

"No? You told me not too long ago that Bors the Elder was not my father. You went on to say that my real father died years ago and the man who had raised me is no one to me."

"That's not what I said."

"Bors the Elder is either my father or he isn't; and both he and yourself have informed me that he isn't."

Merlin took a deep breath as if he was about to say a thousand words at once.

"I said you were the son of Uther Pendragon, Duke of Drachenheim whom I took from your mother Igrain for your safety. That doesn't mean Bors the Elder wasn't your father."

"Is this some sort of joke to you?" Arthur said dropping the wood to the floor.

"Who gave you your first riding lessons when you were a child?" Merlin asked. "Who taught you how to read, how to write and carpentry?"

These questions stunned Arthur for a moment.

"Who took you fishing and hunting? Who taught you the sword and the bow? And who has been teaching you how to be a man since the time you first realized that there is a difference between boys and girls?"

Arthur felt as if being attacked by an enemy and wanted to retaliate. However, there was truth in those words he couldn't deny.

"The only real contribution to your life that Uther has made are a name and a few feverish moments. Bors the Elder has raised you as his own and has worked hard to ensure you are as good and righteous of a man as he is.

"Not only is he your father in all the ways that are real and important, he's been a better father to you than any man in this world. I don't always choose wisely; but in placing you in the hands of that loving, fair and just man, I've never made a better decision."

Arthur then felt the strength in his legs start to leave him and he sat down also feeling the weight of the world pressing down on his shoulders. Still hearing all of his questions screaming in his head, he heard him ask only one.

"Why did I try to lift that blasted sword?"

"Because you were meant to," Merlin told him in a voice that seemed to echo from all around him. "One day or another the path of your life would have led to Excalibur's resting place."

Arthur rubbed his face as if to physically rub the questions out of his mind.

"Sounds like you're about to tell me that it's my destiny to be King," He said to the Wizard.

"That's one possible destiny," Merlin answered.

"You mean there are more than one?" Arthur asked almost like a joke. He felt an attempt at being funny might defuse the discussion enough for the Wizard to go away.

"Everyone in this world has a thousand possible destinies," Merlin told him. "It is the decisions that we make that decide greatness or being forgotten by history."

Arthur looked at the Wizard incredulously. He was starting to tire of the sorcerer and wasn't in the mood for riddles.

"That makes absolutely no sense whatsoever," He told Merlin.

"Not now," Merlin answered. "But in time it will become clear. We all are gifted with a combination of natural gifts and circumstances that can mold us into one potential or another; some more than others. You've been gifted with plenty to make you a strong and wise King, but it won't happen to you. You have to make it happen by the way you choose to utilize your particular gifts."

"And what makes you think I'll decide to be King?" Arthur asked as he looked to where he thought Merlin should be. Unfortunately, the Wizard was gone just as suddenly as he'd arrived.

Arthur felt frustrated by Merlin's disappearance, but then like a whisper in his ear, he heard Merlin's voice tell him, "Because in time not only will you feel that you want to be King, you will feel that you have to be."

More Visitors

It was dark when Arthur decided to join his guests and the servants. One of the servants had set out a torch outside the door of the room in which he had been working and he followed the corridors and staircases toward the dim light he assumed was where the others were waiting on him.

The great spiral staircase that led down to the great hall seemed a little more fragile as it was bathed in a slightly orange hue.

Before going around the bend in the stairs, he could clearly hear the voice of Bors the Elder speaking to someone and two familiar voices laughed evidently at a joke he'd told.

Just before reaching the bottom of the steps, Arthur saw the large fire pit in the center of the hall ablaze and four men sitting around it. Looking closely, he was pleasantly surprised to see that the two newcomers were none other than his friends Gawain and Betivere.

"You've had a bath recently," Betivere called up to him. "Thank God for that."

"What the bloody hell are you two doing here?" Arthur asked half laughing.

"Looking for you," Gawain answered. "When we found you were gone from the hill we thought you'd been carried off by a dragon. We knew perfectly well you hadn't run away."

"And what made you think that?" Arthur asked.

"You're not smart enough to run away from anything," Betivere answered.

Arthur greeted and embraced his friends and asked, "How the devil did you know to find me here?"

"We followed those two," Gawain answered pointing at the two Bors'.

"What do you mean 'we'?" Betivere joked. "You can't even follow a paved road, much less track anyone."

"Very funny scab face. I'll have you know that I've tracked deer for days without losing them."

"I thought the objective was to kill the deer before you had to track it for days," Betivere joked and then Arthur had to step in between them again. It was just like old times.

"So what happened?" Arthur asked later.

The servants had provided a fine dinner for all five of them complete with plenty of wine and beer.

"The last thing I remember was that Uriants and Leon des Gras were about to come to blows."

"They very nearly did," Bors the Elder said. "The crowd was starting to line up against each other as well."

"So what happened next?"

"We have no idea," Betivere answered. "One moment all hell is about to break loose; the next thing we know we're all waking up strewn across the hill and feeling like our heads had been trampled on."

"Merlin's doing no doubt," Gawain added.

"I suspect this is all his doing," Bors the Younger said.

"Not all of it," the man Arthur had previously known as his father told everyone.

His eyes met with Arthur's in what looked like an apology.

"Arthur was always meant to have the Sword," the Elder Bors told them all. "I never knew it until Arthur drew the Sword from the stone."

"What did you know?" Arthur said with a hint of anger in his voice.

All eyes looked to Bors the Elder who paused and tried to tell the story as truthfully, yet gently as he could.

"That you were an orphan," He finally started saying, "And that I was never to speak of Merlin having brought you to me. I never knew…" he tried to say, but found himself getting choked up.

Arthur saw tears welling up in his eyes and told Bors "It's alright" gently so that the proud man wouldn't cry.

He felt that the legendary Knight had already suffered enough embarrassment. While the other three around him might not care, Bors himself would have felt humiliated in losing control over his emotions in front of others.

"So when did you arrive?" Arthur asked Gawain and Betivere.

"Not more than two hours ago," Betivere answered. "We were going to try and get a room at an inn in Camelot, but the old woman chased us into the manor with a spoon."

"I did no such thing!" The voice of Elsbeth shouted at them. "And I'm not so old that I can't put over my knee!"

"I might be a bit young for that," Betivere replied. "But I think this older gentleman here might be up to the challenge."

"Why you miserable little..."

She started to come at Betivere with a large spoon, but Arthur stopped her.

"Don't take it personally Elsbeth," Arthur told her. "The worse of an insult one gets from Betivere, the more of a compliment it is."

"You should hear the things he's said about his own mother," Gawain chuckled.

"Which reminds me," Betivere told Gawain, "You still owe her ten gold."

Elsbeth gasped in horror while the five men all laughed.

After they'd all drank at least three full flagons of beer, Arthur noticed the eyes of Bors the Younger staring off past them and following someone's movement. He turned to see what Bors must have been following and saw Rachel going back and forth across the hall, occasionally looking at Bors and smiling at him.

"There's that thunderclap again," Betivere said with a broad smile.

"What do you mean?" Bors the Younger asked attempting to sound innocent.

"It's the unmistakable sound of a young man falling desperately in love with a girl he's not even spoken with yet."

"I don't know what you're talking about," Bors the Younger huffed and returned to staring at the fire.

"Nothing to be embarrassed about son," the older Bors told his son. "It happens to us all."

"Some more than others," Betivere added with a grin. "Surely you must have heard it when poor Arthur first saw that lovely creature back at the camp."

"I think the whole Land heard it," Gawain joked. "What was her name again?"

"I don't know what you're talking about," Arthur told them, though he knew they could likely see the smile on his face he couldn't hide.

"Guinevere," Betivere said as if saying the name of a goddess, "The lovely daughter of Leon des Gras. How many armed and dangerous brothers does she have?"

"At last count, she had eight," Bors the Elder answered. "All sworn to protect her honor to their own death; though it's more likely they'll defend it to the death of anyone who ventures too close."

"I'm sure Arthur can take at least one of them down," Gawain said chuckling.

"Will any of you help me with the other seven?" Arthur asked.

"Good God no!" Betivere answered.

The five of them drank and talked well into the night. When the beer finally ran out, Arthur decided against trying to climb the stairs back to his room.

He was drunk but not so much as to actually think he could climb the steps without falling to his death.

The servants brought down pillows and blankets for them all to sleep on and even Betivere sincerely expressed his gratitude.

Arthur often found it ironic that Betivere was less obnoxious drunk than sober. He also talked a lot more. In fact, the last thing Arthur remembered from the night was Betivere still droning on and on about his bees.

The following morning, Arthur winced as bright sunlight seemed to sting him in the eyes. His head started feeling as if someone had run a sword through it and the groaning from the others sounded like thunder.

"Come on gentlemen," Elsbeth's voice echoed off of the stone walls. "You've already slept through most of the morning and neither Ascher nor Rachel can get any of our work done until you're off of your backs."

Still groaning and feeling a hundred pounds heavier Arthur asked, "Were you this cruel with your former master?"

"Hmph!" Elsbeth snorted. "Lord Uther would have never let you sleep past the dawn, much less half the day."

"No wonder they murdered him," Betivere said under his breath.

"I heard that!" Elsbeth shouted from across the hall.

Arthur and the others ate breakfast and started to resign themselves to the reality that they were going to have to help the servants collect all the dead from the castle; otherwise it would take weeks to accomplish. Being surrounded by bones in empty clothing was unsettling to everyone.

Both Gawain and Bors the Elder complimented the servants to Arthur. Although Arthur did say how much he valued them, he had to admit that he doubted that would be able to keep them.

"They're wonderful people," Arthur told Bors. "Unless gold coins start falling from the sky, I'm going to have to let them go."

"Don't you worry about money," Ascher told him.

Arthur then noticed both Ascher and Elsbeth look at each other as if both had a secret they were sharing.

Gawain was having more trouble than anyone waking up. His eyes were heavy and his legs kept threatening to give way at any moment. He stepped up to Betivere and told him, "Slap me."

"I beg your pardon," Betivere told him in disbelief.

"I'm serious," Bors told him. "I can't wake up. I need you to slap me across the face."

"You're serious aren't you?"

"Will you just shut up and hit me?"

"Fine," Betivere sighed and then struck him across the face.

Gawain sighed and said to Betivere, "You call that a strike? My grandmother hits harder than that and she's dead. For God's sake hit me!"

Bors the Elder than punched him hard and Gawain fell to the ground with a thud.

"How's that?" Bors asked as Gawain lay crumpled on the ground.

"Much better, thank you."

A few moments later, Ascher entered the hall and said to Arthur, "You have a visitor My Lord."

Arthur thought briefly about asking Ascher to stop calling him "My Lord," but then his curiosity took over.

"Are you expecting anyone?" Gawain asked him as he stood up rubbing his chin.

"I was just about to ask you the same question," Arthur answered.

Arthur followed Ascher to the entrance hall and was surprised to see the merchant from the day before standing in front of him. The man was alone, but Arthur was still wary. It was then that he noticed that Excalibur was in his hand again and he thought to himself that this was starting to get annoying.

Arthur was about to unleash several harsh words in the merchant's direction when the man did what was likely the last thing Arthur expected. He fell to one knee and bowed in Arthur's direction.

"My Lord Arthur," the merchant said reverently. "We need your help."

And Then They Said "Please"

Arthur heard Gawain and Betivere approach from behind and they saw an expression on Arthur's face that gave them the impression that Arthur may have thought he was in a dream.

"You do see this right?" Arthur asked his two friends.

"I certainly see it," Gawain answered. "But I can't honestly say I believe it."

"Would you like me to pinch you to see if it's a dream?" Betivere asked.

"You do and being half blind will be the least of your disabilities," Arthur answered turning back to the merchant.

"This is a rather sudden change of tune," He said to the still-kneeling merchant.

The merchant then bowed his head again in deference to Arthur.

"I sincerely and whole-heartedly apologize for my behavior yesterday morning," The merchant pleaded. "Upon my soul, I swear that I will never behave that way again."

Arthur looked to Betivere, who always seemed to be able to understand people better than anyone present in a given situation. It was even rumored that, like Lord Uriants he could smell a lie.

"He sounds pretty sincere to me," Betivere told Arthur.

Arthur looked at Gawain who merely shrugged his shoulders and then back at the merchant who was wearing a desperate and pleading expression on his face.

"So what is it that's caused such a change of heart?" Arthur asked.

"My Lord," the merchant began. "Five nights ago, five men dressed as soldiers came to the inn that my brother keeps. They were very rude to everyone, loud, boastful and whenever anyone looked them in the eyes, they'd threaten them. We all thought we could put up with them for just a day or so, but it's been five days now. When my brother tried to speak to them about their bill, they beat him and then threw him into a cess pit."

"That doesn't sound very friendly," Betivere mumbled.

"They've trashed my brother's inn, drank all of his beer and most of his wine, completely cleaned out his panty, destroyed the beds and other furniture in their rooms and then to make matters worse, one of them…"

At this point he paused and looked like he was starting to get sick.

"Go on," Arthur urged.

The merchant looked as though he was searching for just the right words.

"Well…," he tried, "My brother…"

"Yes?"

"Well…he has this…goat…"

"Never mind," Arthur said quickly. "I'm better off not knowing the rest."

"Please, My Lord. You simply must do something. My brother has a wife and children. He's been injured so badly that he won't able to work for weeks. Repairing the damage will cost so much, he won't be able to afford a doctor…"

"Yes, I get the picture," Arthur interrupted. "Where are they now?"

"They're still at the inn and have stated that they have no intention of leaving."

"And how many of them did you say there were?"

"Five, My Lord."

Arthur looked to Gawain and he appeared to have been angered by the story they'd just told. Arthur reminded himself that Gawain was typically very easy to anger; but stories that involved innocent people being harmed tended to affect him the most.

"How long has it been since you've been in a fight?" Arthur asked Gawain.

"Not since the 'Tavern Brawl'."

"Poor lad," Betivere interjected. "He must be starving."

"My Lord," the merchant said in an even more desperate voice, "My people promise to give you their most sincere loyalty if you'll take care of this situation for us."

"What do you think?" Arthur asked his friends.

It's not every day that a city the size of Camelot offers their undying loyalty," Betivere answered.

"It does sound better than pitchforks and torches," Arthur added.

He then looked to Gawain who was now wearing his unmistakable expression of gleefully anticipating a good fight.

"Alright then," Arthur said to the merchant, "Go back to Camelot and tell your people that I'll be about half an hour behind you."

The merchant then leapt forward and returning to one knee, took Arthur's hand and started kissing it. Arthur was a little startled by this and in an instant felt Excalibur in his hand again.

Arthur told Bors the Elder and his son where he was going and was almost out of the main entrance when Elsbeth stood blocking him holding what appeared to be a small bundle in her hands.

"Whatever it is," He told her, "It's going to have to wait. I'm in a little bit of a hurry right now."

Elsbeth then held out the bundle to Arthur and he then saw that it was a suit of chainmail and a black tunic with the five dragon symbol on the chest.

"You're the Duke of Drachenheim now," she told him. "It's time the rest of the world came to know who you are."

Arthur examined the uniform carefully and noted, "I think these may be a bit large for me."

"Nonsense, My Lord," She told him proudly. "There is no one else that could possibly wear this. In fact, you may prove to be too big for them."

Arthur dressed himself and then almost ran out of the manor again. Elsbeth intercepted him again; this time holding what looked like a leather purse.

"You may need some money," She told him.

He opened the purse and was shocked to see how many pure gold coins were inside.

"Good Lord!" He exclaimed.

"This should get you by for a few days."

"That's more money than I've seen in all my life."

"There's plenty more where that came from too, My Lord."

Arthur thought for a second about questioning her about it, but then remembered that he had somewhere very important to go.

"We'll discuss this when I get back," he told her and then raced out of the main entrance. At the bottom of the stone steps, Severus was already waiting for him.

Camelot

It took less than half an hour for Arthur and Gawain to ride from the castle to Camelot. Once there, Arthur wished he hadn't left Dragonhearth.

Everything he'd previously read about Camelot told of golden cobblestones, wide streets and boulevards, the "delicious aromas" of exotic foods and beverages and "Music coming from every door and window" was gone. What he found instead were closed doors and windows, run-down buildings, faces of fear and only the aroma of open sewage.

He could feel the eyes of everyone in the city watching him, but very few were on the streets. The faces he did see in windows quickly vanished behind shutters slamming shut.

"This is Camelot?" Arthur heard himself ask.

"She's not what she once was," the merchant Arthur now knew as Saul told him. "After the death of the King, every thief and murderer in the Land came through these streets destroying everything they couldn't take with them."

"Was there no one to defend these streets?" Gawain asked.

"The retainer Knights that once served Uther that weren't butchered either took part in the scourging of Drachenheim or simply disappeared. No one's cared to defend this city for many years."

The streets widened and Arthur could tell that there was greatness in this city once. But the buildings and homes of those who had stayed were mostly falling down from disrepair and neglect.

The city he rode through now looked as though a hundred years had passed since the death of Uther and every building around him had the feel of a funeral.

After they rounded one corner in the center of the city, Arthur could hear loud and drunken voices coming from a small building at the end of the street.

"Those must be your visitors," Arthur said to Saul.

"Yes My Lord," the merchant answered.

"Why didn't you tell me about this yesterday?"

"Bergeron, the owner of the inn didn't mention it to me until this morning. He was afraid that if he even tried to get a message to anyone, he'd be killed."

With a simple nod, Arthur acknowledged that this made sense.

There were five horses parked at the front of the inn and all five of them appeared to be abused and starved. They all hung their heads low and sadness seemed to spill from their eyes.

This made Arthur even angrier as having cared for animals most of his life, he hated the very thought of any beast being made to suffer intentionally or otherwise. This was something he simply had to rectify.

He and Gawain dismounted and as his foot touched the ground, he thought he could actually hear the strangers' horses pleading for his help. He rubbed the neck of one of the saddest ones as if to reassure him that his days of suffering were nearly over.

Peering in through the open doorway, he saw the five men sitting at a table in the center of the inn's open hall. They were all seated around a large table with cards in their hands and stacks of coins in front of each one of them along with dozens of empty flagons and wine bottles.

"Where's that damn wine I ordered not half an hour ago?" One of them shouted.

He was by far the largest one of them. His armor and tunic barely clung to his massive body. His face was pitted and scarred from long ago battles and a thick beard glistening from spilled beer and wine covered his mouth.

The other four were barely clinging to consciousness as they were upright in the chairs only with much effort. Their only expression came from sickening laughter at every vulgar utterance to spill from their master's mouth as he spewed one obscenity after another.

There were others in the tavern as well, but every time one of them would move, the fat beast would shout at him or her, "Where the hell do you think you're going? I said no one leaves this inn and I damn well mean it!"

"I don't know about you," Gawain told Arthur, "But I think I've seen enough."

"Alright then," Arthur replied. "Let's get this over with."

"Where's that god damned wine?" The beast bellowed. "If I have to ask again, I'll slice someone's head off and I don't care whose head it is!"

Arthur watched as a young girl that reminded him of Guinevere quickly brought a bottle of wine over to the men. The obese one grabbed the girl and sat her in his lap.

"Come on girl," he laughed. "Give us a kiss!"

She struggled with him a moment and then finally wrestled away from him. As she escaped, he managed to tear off a piece of her dress.

"Don't worry lass," he shouted. "I'll be here when you want more!"

All five followed this with even more sickening laughter.

Arthur maneuvered past the overturned and broken tables and chairs and then to within less than a foot from the beast in his chair. At first, the disgusting man paid no attention to him. However, as Arthur continued to stare angrily at him, he eventually spoke to him.

"Something on your mind boy?" The beast gurgled.

At first Arthur said nothing.

"You keep staring at me, I'm certain to become annoyed."
The beast chuckled at this and his companions as well. Again,
Arthur did not respond.

"I think you'd better run home to your mother before something
bad happens."

Arthur neither moved nor spoke; instead he waited until Gawain
was on the other side of the table.

"Are you hard of hearing boy?" The beast growled again.

"It is rather difficult to hear you with your mother's moans from
last night still ringing in my ears," Arthur finally told him.

The disgusting man's eyes bulged and he dropped his cards.

"What did you just say to me?" He hissed at Arthur.

"I believe I was trying to tell you that your mother didn't have
enough to pay me for my services last night," Arthur answered. "She
suggested I collect the rest from you."

The beast stumbled out of his chair and then stood menacingly
over Arthur.

"You may not recognize her when you get home," Arthur told
him. "I shaved her back."

The disgusting former Knight then reached for his sword, but before he could draw it, Arthur hit him with four punches to the gut and then to the face sending him plummeting to the ground. At the same time Gawain easily dispatched three of the Knight's companions.

The big one tried to scramble to his feet, but Arthur sent him back to the floor with a heavy kick to the ribs.

Gawain sensed someone behind him and turned just in time to see the last of the unwanted patrons bringing an empty wine bottle towards his head. He easily ducked the attack. And then he grabbed the back of the man's neck and brought his face crashing into his knee.

As the leader of this group rolled onto the floor and moaned in pain, Arthur clearly saw the insignia on his tunic. To his further disgust, he saw that it was the five dragons of Drachenheim. Arthur then kicked him one last time across the face and the Knight fell silent.

For the next several moments and to the cheering of those brave enough to witness the event for themselves, Arthur and Gawain dragged all five men out of the inn and threw them into the excrement that had accumulated behind their horses.

Arthur and Gawain then dumped buckets of water on them to wake them up.

The largest one then finally managed to get to his feet and draw his sword.

"You miserable little pup!" He screamed at Arthur. "You've made the last mistake you'll make in your lifetime!"

Arthur then saw a surprised, almost scared expression on his face and it didn't take long for Arthur to understand where the look had come from. Excalibur was in his hand again, despite Arthur having intentionally left it back at the castle.

Arthur then saw the beast regain some courage and point his sword directly at both Arthur and Gawain.

"Enjoy this victory for now," the big one groaned, "But know that it will be your last. I have a dozen men waiting for me in the woods outside this city. We'll be back tonight and burn this city to the ground!"

"I look forward to it," Arthur told him haughtily. "But if you do return tonight, be aware that I will show you no such mercy as I have shown this morning. If you return to my city either tonight or any night, I will happily dispatch you to the gates of hell that await you!"

The men started to move to mounting their horses, but Arthur and Gawain stopped them.

"Consider them part of the bill you owe," Gawain growled.

"But how are we supposed to…" One of them tried to speak.

Gawain merely replied with a menacing stare. As the big one and his companions marched away from the inn, the big one turned once more and warned Arthur, "This is your last day on this Earth, boy!"

With the people of Camelot showering them with curses, rotting food and excrement, the five men abandoned the city.

"Do you think he was serious about a dozen men in the woods?" Gawain asked Arthur.

"To be safe, I think we should assume that he is," Arthur answered.

Arthur then looked around for something he wasn't quite sure of and then saw a tall boy with a face far younger than his height.

"What's your name?" He asked the lad.

"Kyle sir," the boy answered.

Arthur fished out a gold coin and gave it to the youth telling him, "Go up to the castle and tell the old woman that I need the others to join me here before sundown."

"What others, sir?"

"Never mind that, just tell her please."

"How am I to get there?"

Arthur thought momentarily of reminding the youth that his legs were clearly not broken, but decided instead to help him on to Severus.

"Whoa!" the boy exclaimed excitedly. "Is this my horse now?"

"Only in your dreams lad," Arthur answered.

Gawain then stood next to Arthur and asked him quietly, "Five of us against twelve of them?"

"You're right," Arthur replied and then told Gawain; "Tell the old woman to send Betivere and Bors the Younger only."

He didn't need to tell Severus or the other horses what to do as all of them departed with the boy yelling happily and wildly.

Arthur then saw the confused expression on Gawain's face and told him, "I doubt there are enough of them to go around."

The Duke of Drachenheim

Bors the Younger and Betivere arrived less than two hours after Arthur sent the young boy Kyle to summon them. At Arthur's request, Betivere was sent towards the distant woods in order to determine if there really were "a dozen" soldiers or Knights waiting in the woods or if it was just a bluff.

While they were waiting for Betivere to return, the staff of the inn made it a point to try and thank Arthur and Gawain as best as they could.

At one point, the young girl who worked for the inn brought them both bowls of soup. With a sad, yet hopeful look in her eyes, she told them both "I'm sorry, but this is all we have."

"This is perfectly fine," Arthur told her and while they were eating both Arthur and Gawain went out of their way to demonstrate how delicious the soup was and how much they both appreciated it.

"This is the best soup I've ever had," Gawain said at one point.

"Oh yes," Arthur added. "You should send this up to the castle as often as possible."

The girl smiled brightly and practically danced away from the two of them.

"You weren't serious were you?" Gawain whispered to Arthur.

"Just keep smiling and eating your soup," Arthur told him sternly.

One by one, various citizens of the city came into the inn offering what little they had to the man they had heard was their new Duke.

As they did, they told of the troubles they'd had since the death of Uther and the dark times that followed.

They spoke of thieves and villains going in and out of the once great city and visiting one catastrophe after another upon them.

Merchants and traders spoke of trade drying up and the citizens barely surviving on mere scraps of food and drink. The inn had managed to stay open because Saul and his brother Goran had braved the forty mile journey between Camelot and Elderol, the next closest town in order to bring back beer, wine and food.

More than once, they'd been assailed by thieves on the road and they weren't always successful at fending them off.

They spoke of fires that had consumed whole streets, buildings washed away in floods and whole herds of livestock dying of disease.

Arthur listened to all of these carefully and tried to show no emotion, but it was difficult. Each painful story had Arthur feeling a sample of the agony each citizen of this once great city knew.

"So what do you intend to do about all of this?" Saul asked Arthur at one point.

"I honestly don't know," Arthur told him flatly. "But whatever can be done will be done. One thing you must all understand is that whatever it is that we are able to do, we will have to start with the most needy first."

The people who had crammed into the inn all mumbled either in agreement or disappointment and Arthur hoped that would be the end of depressing news for the day.

"What do you mean we?" Gawain asked.

"I was referring to myself and the people who've been sleeping in my castle and eating my food without paying for it."

"Hmph…" Gawain snorted. "Didn't take you long to start acting like a proper Duke."

The young girl then put two more full bowls of her soup in front of Arthur and Gawain and they both gave her their most sincere attempts at smiling. Fortunately for them, Betivere returned from his reconnoiter.

"Well?" Arthur asked him.

"Oh they're out there alright," Betivere answered. "They're so ripe, I'm surprised you can't smell them in here."

"How far away?" Gawain asked.

"Three miles."

"How close did you get?" Arthur then asked.

"Close enough that I could hear their plans."

"Anything I need to know about?"

"They plan to leave their encampment at midnight so they can attack while they assume everyone is asleep."

"That's about five hours from now," Bors the Younger added.

"Their leader said he wanted to rest up before beginning the march here," Betivere went on. "And you should have heard the things he planned to do with you, Arthur."

"Yes, I'm sure I'll be the highlight of the evening."

"So what are we going to do?" Gawain asked.

Arthur sighed and shrugged his shoulders.

"For now," he said, "We're going to wait until it's completely dark and then we're going to put a final end to this nonsense."

"What are we supposed to do in the meantime?" Betivere then asked.

Arthur then handed him a bowl and told him, "Have some soup."

That night as the silvery full moon shown through thin clouds, Arthur, Gawain, Betivere and Bors rode to the edge of the woods.

There they left Severus in charge of the horses and crept through the woods in search of their prey. In order to move as quietly as possible, they wore no armor and only carried one weapon each so as to move as quickly as possible.

Arthur was never particularly fond of the heavy armor that Knights wore anyway. The only purpose the armor filled he thought was to slow people down and make more noise.

Bors the Elder had taught both his son Bors and Arthur how to fight without armor and the added speed and maneuverability gave them an edge against heavily laden foes.

It didn't take long to find the light of the marauders campfire shining in the woods. Arthur could hear the big one's voice booming over the others and he continued to describe in detail all the horrible things he was going to do with the "Insolent worm" who had dared assault him.

"By the time I'm done with him," Arthur heard the big one say, "He'll wish his father had never set eyes on his mother. I'm going to pull his liver out of his belly, fry it up and eat it while he watches in agony."

"I can't wait to get my hands on that bearded one," another said excitedly.

"I'm going to make him squeal like a pig while I defile him in front of everyone in that city."

"Don't get too attached to the city," The big one warned. "By tomorrow morning it will be nothing but a pile of ash."

While this discussion was going on, Arthur and his companions took positions behind the men. They were close enough to feel the heat of the fire, but still hidden in the shadows.

Arthur found their horses and untied them from the trees securing them. They all seemed grateful to be released and needed no encouragement to leave.

With the thieve's means of escape having been eliminated, Arthur concluded that it was time to get to work. He stepped out from the trees and practically into the flames of the campfire itself. The thieves were shocked and for a moment seemed paralyzed.

"Tell me again," Arthur said to the big one, "Were you intending to fry my liver or boil it in oil?"

The moment they all started scrambling to their feet, Gawain, Bors and Betivere rushed into the circle. Bors cut down two foes as he charged in and swung his sword at his enemy. Gawain brought the pummel of his sword crashing down on the skull of another and then in seemingly the same motion, dispatched another charging him.

Betivere spun and whirled like a dancer with four of the thieves surrounding him. He pulled his own sword out from the staff so quickly, two of his foes never saw it even after he'd opened huge gashes in their flesh.

The staff in Betivere's left hand split the skull of the third and the fourth tried to run, but only ran into the blade of Excalibur waiting for him. Within mere seconds eight bodies laid silently on the ground.

The big one got to his feet and held up a huge battle axe. He brought it down in one mighty motion against Arthur's sword expecting to knock it out of the seemingly weaker man's hands as he'd done in countless battle before.

To his horror, he saw his axe shatter like glass against the gleaming steel and almost fell over backwards in his reaction.

One thief had managed to get behind Arthur and started to swing a mace at Arthur's head. He would never know whether his blow would strike or not as Arthur almost casually swung Excalibur behind him and silenced him forever.

Looking at the big one panic and try to crawl away from him, Arthur felt almost mad with anger. He wanted to destroy this foul beast utterly, slashing him blindly and letting the Sword do its worst.

Just before letting his rage burst from within, he stopped himself. Bors the Elder had taught him to never give in to blind rage. He found a little bit of calm in a deep, cleansing breath and regained his focus.

He then kicked the disgusting beast hard in the ribs causing him to roll over.

"First of all," Arthur said to the creature, "You'll not be needing this."

With the Sword, Arthur ripped the tunic off of the big one's body.

"If my father could see what had become of someone he'd once trusted to wear his colors, he'd never be half as merciful as I'm going to be."

The big one looked at Arthur in desperate horror and looking in his face, he saw the image of his former master, Uther Pendragon.

"No," he gasped. "It can't be. Uther had no son."

Arthur then kicked him across the face.

"Silence you worm!" Arthur shouted at him. "I'm not finished with you yet!"

Arthur then stepped on the beast's neck to demonstrate his total power over the wretch. He then felt a surge of energy wash through him like a powerful ocean wave.

"Listen to me very carefully," Arthur growled at the sickening creature beneath him. "I am Arthur, son of Uther Pendragon, Duke of Drachenheim. Before sunrise, you will leave my lands and never return."

"Y...yes...My Lord," the beast stammered.

"Furthermore," Arthur continued grimly. "You will tell all who mean to defile the lands under my control to steer as far from Drachenheim as possible as there is only death for them to find here."

"Ye...yes My Lord. I'll tell them."

"Now to the last. If I ever so much as hear of you being within my borders again, I will visit upon you so much terror, you will gladly welcome death."

The thief nodded and promised that Arthur would never see him again. Arthur then slashed the thief across the face, telling him, "That's so you'll remember this night for the rest of your miserable life."

When Arthur released the thief, he scrambled to his feet and ran faster than Arthur thought someone of that girth capable. He then turned to his friends and saw expressions he'd never seen in them before.

They looked shocked, but also in awe. It was almost as if they saw one of the old gods of the woods and streams standing before them. Arthur looked at them quizzically and then asked, "What?"

More Work to Do

The very first thing Arthur did when returning to Dragonhearth Castle was ask Elsbeth to tell him where she had gotten more gold than Arthur had ever seen in his life.

Elsbeth then dutifully led him to the family crypt behind the castle and specifically to the very last tomb.

Overlooking the effigy of Duke Oldum was a relief of a dragon carved into the wall. She pressed two fingers into the eyes of the dragon and then the entire wall slid open.

Led inside, Arthur nearly fainted when he saw a cave nearly fifty feet square and having a ceiling twenty feet high almost completely filled with gold, silver, jewels and other treasures.

"Good Lord!" Arthur exclaimed when seeing the treasure within the cave. "There's enough here to last a lifetime!"

"More like twenty lifetimes, My Lord," Elsbeth answered.

While lying in bed with Rachel curled up next to him (she was evidently making a habit of sleeping next to Arthur), Arthur contemplated how much his life had changed in seemingly the blink of an eye.

He found out that the family he'd always known were not tied to him by blood. He'd read the story of Merlin taking a baby from the arms of Lady Igrain of Cornwall, but never dreamed the story referred to him.

Did Bors the Elder lie to him all of these years? While contemplating this, Arthur couldn't remember ever asking the man he'd known as "Father" his entire life if he really was Bors' son.

Why should I, he wondered? Who even thinks to ask that kind of question of the only parents they'd ever known?

He still had the visions of the beautiful woman crying in despair, but he couldn't determine if this was a real memory or simply something his imagination had conjured.

Everything he'd seen and heard since (somehow) arriving at Dragonhearth seemed to reinforce the notion that he was, in fact the Duke of Drachenheim by his birthright. Even Bors the Elder acknowledged enough of the story for it to be true.

But in a very short time, he'd gone from a simple squire looking forward to managing the family farm to a Duke not having the slightest idea of how to rule.

The people in Camelot seemed perfectly willing to acknowledge him as the Duke, but he also knew that Camelot was not the only place in his land that needed convincing. And how exactly was he supposed to rule these lands? What was expected of him?

In his thoughts, he concluded that he couldn't just declare himself Duke and expect the people of Drachenheim to bow down before him. He further concluded that he'd need to earn their loyalty somehow, but he was unsure as to how to do it.

And there was another thing troubling him as well. By drawing Excalibur from the stone, he was supposedly King. However, he knew quite well that he could never simply ask the Lords and Knights of the Land to give him his loyalty.

Lord Uriants certainly wasn't likely to offer his loyalty and though Leon des Gras seemed willing when he last saw him, it had apparently been almost three whole months since that day on the hill. By now, it was most likely he'd changed his mind.

Betivere, the son and heir apparent to the Earl of Sunderland was here with him. However, Betivere was not yet the Earl. Would their friendship be changed by the circumstances that had changed?

Gawain seemed a safer bet. However, he'd been knighted by Lord Uriants and was also the nephew of Lady Igrain. Where were his true loyalties?

As so often happens, an idea came to him just as he falling into sleep. The one idea connected with several others and by the time he felt an actual plan emerge from his thoughts, he had to also acknowledge that he wouldn't be able to sleep until he'd at least started on making his plan a reality.

The very first thing he did after the sun had risen was rouse all of his "guests" by gently nudging (kicking) them on the butts.

"I certainly hope this castle's burning to the ground," Betivere told him. "Otherwise, I'm not prepared to even think of getting off my rump."

"Come on, you lazy freeloaders," Arthur told them all. "We've got work to do."

Before noon, Arthur set up a makeshift "court" in the inn in Camelot. He invited all the business owners and traders in the city to come forward and tell what they thought needed to be done in order to restore their businesses.

Construction materials were needed, as well as supplies and the restoration of trade with other towns and villages.

Arthur asked them for estimates of how much it would cost for the changes and improvements to be implemented. No matter how ridiculous the claim seemed to be, Arthur agreed to pay it.

Arthur also agreed to give each citizen of Camelot an allotment of one hundred in gold to support them until trade and business could be restored.

The biggest obstacle to the restoration of Camelot's economy was the main road leading from Camelot to Elderol. Not only was the road in disrepair, thieves and bandits lined the road waiting for any travelers they could prey upon. This, for Arthur would turn out to be the easy part.

For the first several weeks under Arthur's rule, he sent at least two of his friends onto the road every day to lure bandits and thieves to them. Each attempt at a robbery resulted in the dispatch or one or more criminals.

After two months, the body count had risen to at least twenty. Arthur then sent merchants and traders to Elderol and before long, supplies, materials, food and other essentials began flowing into Camelot.

In due time, things that hadn't been seen in Camelot since Uther Pendragon was alive began coming into the city and merchants and traders in Elderol were starting to send money to Camelot for the goods its citizens were producing again.

Arthur was concerned about the relative security of his Duchy as neither he nor his friends could be everywhere at once. He also knew that his friends couldn't stay forever as all of them had obligations elsewhere.

It was Bors the Elder that came up with a solution to this problem. At his suggestion, Arthur sent word throughout Drachenheim for men to be trained in civil defense and law enforcement.

Fortunately, the previous Dukes had already established a code of law long before Uther became the Duke. The only thing required of the new men was to become familiar with the law and trained in enforcing it.

Less than two weeks after Arthur's invitation, fifty men arrived at Dragonhearth and Bors immediately set about the task of training them.

The idea was that these men, once trained would go to assigned locations throughout the Duchy, establish themselves as Sheriffs and/or magistrates and they, and in turn would train others in basic combat and weaponry.

Arthur was well aware that there may be a time when he may need to raise an army for one reason or another. It would be better if this potential army had soldiers that were already trained, rather than see untrained and unprepared soldiers slaughtered by professional soldiers such as Lord Uriants' standing army.

Within a month, life began flowing back into Camelot. Two more roads were cleared of criminals and made safe for trade. Artisans and craftsmen began making things that the people of other towns and villages wanted from Camelot and more money started flowing in and out of Camelot than had been seen in over a decade.

Men trained in the prevention of crime and law enforcement went on to their stations and Arthur eventually started receiving word that they were mostly welcome and their work appreciated.

In just under a year, Arthur transformed the once devastated Duchy into a thriving land of peace and commerce.

On one crisp, yet clear day, Arthur and other workers were making repairs to a boarding house in the center of Camelot.

It was Early-November and although Drachenheim had been blessed with relatively mild weather, Arthur knew the winter snows were coming.

It was imperative that as much work as possible be done to ensure the people of Camelot did not suffer another cruel winter in houses and buildings that provided little shelter from the elements.

Practically the entire city needed to be rebuilt. Carpenters and engineers followed the promise of good pay for honest work to Camelot. None of them would be disappointed.

The work was hard; but steady. And the Duke of Drachenheim's pay for their labor was more than fair.

Despite all the gold that had been paid, barely a dent had been made on the hoard in the cave.

One crisp autumn morning, Arthur was busy sanding the sides of wooden planks down to smooth edges so that they would fit better together on a building being renovated.

By doing this himself, Arthur felt he was setting an example and sending a message that only the best quality work would be tolerated. Construction crews from all over Drachenheim came to Camelot once they found out that real money was being paid for the city's rebirth.

Most of these workmen were far superior craftsmen than Arthur, but he still wanted to keep himself busy.

Arthur heard the horse's steps approaching and out of the corner of his eye saw a man in fine linens approaching astride a beautiful, tan mare.

"You there! Carpenter!" The man shouted down to Arthur. "I'm looking for the Duke of Drachenheim."

Feeling slightly annoyed by the interruption of his work, Arthur asked him," What business have you with the Duke?"

"That is none of your affair Carpenter," the man said haughtily. "Now show me to your master before I have you flogged."

This caught Arthur's attention. He turned and glared at the stranger and almost unleashed a torrent of obscenities when Gawain called down from the window of the room he was working in.

"Cyril!" Gawain shouted. "That is the Duke!"

"That," Cyril said with a condescending sneer, "Is the Duke?"

"It most certainly is, you worm and if he doesn't flay you alive for disrespecting him, I will."

Arthur stepped up to the man he now knew as Cyril and asked him, "What business do you have with me? I'm a little bit busy at the moment."

Cyril then took off his hat in a dramatic gesture and bowed before Arthur.

"My Lord Duke," Cyril said grandly. "I bring you greetings from her gracious ladyship, the Duchess of Cornwall."

These words hit Arthur like a slap in the face. The Duchess of Cornwall was none other than the Lady Igrain; the woman who was supposed to be his mother. After a few stunned seconds, Arthur finally managed to ask, "How fares her Ladyship?"

"She is well, My Lord and she has bid me relay a message to you along with her most sincere best wishes."

Arthur had seen the messengers of nobility before relaying messages to Bors the Elder in this dramatic manner. Until that day, he never once thought he would be treated with such courtesy.

"What message is that?" Arthur said trying to wash his hands.

The messenger held a rolled up piece of paper tied with a ribbon. Not entirely sure how to act in such circumstances, Arthur smiled a little, gave a polite bow and took the paper from the messenger.

By this time, Gawain had come downstairs and stood just behind Arthur.

Arthur stood staring at the rolled paper and ribbon not entirely sure what to do with it. Sensing the question Arthur would inevitably ask, Gawain told him, "Open it up and read it."

Arthur carefully undid the ribbon and unrolled the paper. On the paper, written in the beautiful handwriting of an educated lady was an invitation from Lady Igrain.

"My Gracious Lord, Duke of Drachenheim," the invitation began. "I would like to invite yourself and whomever accompanies you to my home at Seacrest in the land of Cornwall. I would be honored if you and yours would join me in celebrating the winter holidays in the comfort of my manor and the company of my precious friends and family."

"Whoa," Gawain moaned. "An invitation by the Duchess herself. Not everyone gets one of those."

Gawain then noticed that Arthur looked a bit stunned, almost frightened by the scrap of paper in his hand.

"What's wrong?" Gawain asked.

"I'm not really sure what to do with this."

"Well, the answer would seem fairly obvious to me," Gawain told him.

"And what is that?"

"You go."

Questions in Need of Answers

The general consensus of everyone at the castle seemed to be that Arthur not only should accept Lady Igrain's invitation; but that it would be utter foolishness not to go. For many years, Lady Igrain had been a virtual recluse behind Seacrest's mighty walls.

In more recent years however, she had become much more open and welcoming and the rare few that were invited to her winter holiday celebration had been rewarded a pleasant, though not particularly exciting couple of weeks enjoying her hospitality.

Arthur knew that ever since the day her child had been taken from her, she'd continued to send her retainer Knights all over the Land in search of her lost child. She'd even offered a reward for her son being found to anyone who could bring the child to her.

Many came to her halls to claim the reward; but according to Gawain, each time a child was proven to be false only embittered her more.

"She's not a person that one could describe as 'happy'," Gawain explained. "After the death of her first husband and the betrayal of Uther and Merlin, she's held nothing but contempt for men."

"Some have tried to court her with the intention of marriage; and most of those men have been exiled from her land."

Gawain would go on to explain that although she was never known to be discourteous or deny her hospitality to anyone, she'd never even once displayed any interest or affection for any man in her presence. She was never cold nor vindictive. She was more sad and morose; each year seeming to only deepen her sorrow.

"She's identified me as the Duke of Drachenheim," Arthur noted.

Bors the Elder indicated that this was a good omen and that he would likely be most welcomed in her manor.

"Be warned," Bors added. "She has a small army of Knights and soldiers around her at all times and they are fiercely loyal. If you know what's good for you, you'll mind your manners."

The same messenger that had brought Igrain's invitation to Arthur also had invitations for Bors and Gawain. Gawain announced his invitation in a voice full of dread.

"It can't be that bad," Arthur slightly teased him.

"I've been to happier funerals than her castle," Gawain explained.

"If we are all going," Bors added, "We'll need to leave as soon as possible. Seacrest isn't exactly around the corner and the weather will soon become decidedly inhospitable."

Once more Arthur couldn't sleep. While Rachel slept quietly, he stared out the open window of his room and past the city. There were lights coming from the city that Arthur hadn't seen when he first arrived and he heard music coming from many different locations within.

He sensed life coming from Camelot that he hadn't first noticed before beginning his renovations and even though he knew that there was much more work needing to be done, he did feel as if he'd accomplished something tangible.

Thinking of all he had achieved up to that point and all the work still needing to be done distracted him for a little while from the uncertainty of what must surely lay ahead of him.

Arthur then heard the familiar smooth and rich voice of Merlin behind him saying, "Surely it can't be that difficult of a decision to make."

"Have you always simply shown up whether welcome or not?" Arthur asked him with a hint of irritation.

"I like to think that I show up when needed, even if not particularly wanted."

Arthur looked behind him and saw Merlin standing in a shadow, giving him a nearly ghostly appearance. Although still irritated by the intrusion into a privacy he'd learned to value, Arthur did decide that he would find some use for the Wizard's presence.

"And what happens if I don't go?" Arthur asked him.

"I'm not a prophet," Merlin told him. "I've never claimed to able to see the future."

"But you know Igrain and likely everyone else that's sure to be within those castle walls. What do you think would likely happen if I didn't go?"

"Well," Merlin said in a matter-of-fact tone, "Ever since taking you from your arms when you were a baby, I haven't exactly been welcome at Seacrest."

"I can understand that."

"She sent you an invitation for a reason, Arthur. Whether that reason is simple curiosity or something more dramatic only she knows."

"Lovely," Arthur grumbled. "I ask a simple question and you're apparently incapable of a straight answer."

"There is no straight answer for the question you've posed. The likely responses to your presence at Seacrest differs according to who will also be in her halls during the holidays. Every single person within her walls adds their own dimensions. As such, I can't give you any real guidance as to what would happen if you did go. However, I can tell you this. This is an important time for you and there are questions you want to ask and answers that you need like an itch you've never been able to scratch. Lady Igrain is not a young woman anymore, though she's lost none of her beauty. The longer you put off seeking the one and only source for the answers you hunger for, the more likely it will become that the source of those answers will no longer be there to ask."

"Are you trying to tell me that she's dying?" Arthur asked.

"Everyone dies," Merlin answered. "But not everyone has the chance to find solutions to the greater mysteries of their lives. Undoubtedly, Lady Igrain has questions for you that are just as profound as the answers you seek. If you don't make use of the opportunity you have now, there's no guarantee you'll ever have another."

Arthur continued to ponder this for a length of time he wasn't sure of. There were indeed questions burning in his mind. However, he knew full well that asking those questions would be far more difficult than he might imagine.

Once more, Arthur went from room to room waking up the others in the castle in a way he was sure wouldn't be appreciated. In one room, he found Bors the Elder and Elsbeth in bed.

After the initial shock of discovering that the two older individuals had intimate desires of their own, he decided to be happy for them at the moment and to never actually speak of it to Bors or anyone else for that matter.

Before the sun had risen, Arthur and those who would be traveling with him had eaten breakfast and prepared themselves for the long journey as best as they could. It was a five day journey to Seacrest and even that was the short way through the woods and rolling hills that formed the border between Drachenheim and Cornwall.

Gawain, Bors, Betivere and Arthur all agreed not to take any tents or cots with them as that would require a cart or wagon that would only slow them down. That morning was colder than any before and they all felt that the sooner they arrived at Seacrest, the happier they'd all be.

Arthur asked Bors the Younger to stay at Dragonhearth and asserted to the man he still felt as his brother that he had his full confidence in his ability to administrate the Duchy in his absence.

The sun was just starting to climb over the distant hills to the east when Arthur stepped out of the main entrance at the top of the stone steps. He had his saddlebags slung over his shoulder and somehow seemed to know that Severus would meet him when the stallion was ready to go.

Bors the Elder sat quietly on the top step smoking a pipe and Arthur decided that this was the best time to settle something that had also kept him awake. When he sat next to Bors, the man he'd known as his father for as long as he could remember seemed to sense that Arthur was troubled about something.

"What's on your mind?" Bors asked Arthur.

"I've been doing some thinking," Arthur told him nervously.

Bors' joke of, "That sounds dangerous" eased some of the tension.

"The past few weeks have been nothing short of remarkable and I'm still having some trouble straightening out the things I've learned recently in my head."

Bors simply nodded and told Arthur, "I think I can imagine that. It's not every day that a man's entire life turns upside down."

"No it isn't," Arthur chuckled.

He then turned to Bors and told him in as strong a voice as he could manage, "I've only had one father in my life."

Bors replied to this with a strong and proud expression.

"I'm sure Uther Pendragon was a good and strong man, but he's never been a part of my life. Whenever I've needed a father, even those times when I didn't think I wanted one, you've always been there. I would very much like it if you could continue to carry out the tasks Uther Pendragon couldn't."

A slight smile crossed Bors' face. He then clasped Arthur on the shoulder and told him, "You're quickly coming to a time in your life where you will no longer need a father's guidance or assistance. However, until you feel that time has come, I will be honored to serve you in any capacity you will allow."

They both shared a nod and a smile, then quickly changed the subject when they felt the emotions flowing between them were becoming uncomfortable.

By the time the sun had completely climbed over the horizon, Arthur, his friends and the man who he still considered his true father were ready to go.

They said their farewells to Arthur's servants and to Bors the Younger and in an instant bounded out of the castle's gates and across the plains toward Cornwall.

Made in the USA
Monee, IL
02 June 2022